THE BEST BAKER IN THE WORLD

THE BEST BAKER IN THE WORLD

RAJA SEN

Illustrations by VISHAL K. BHARADWAJ

PUFFIN BOOKS

An imprint of Penguin Random House

PUFFIN BOOKS

USA | Canada | UK | Ireland | Australia
New Zealand | India | South Africa | China

Puffin Books is part of the Penguin Random House group of companies
whose addresses can be found at global.penguinrandomhouse.com

Published by Penguin Random House India Pvt. Ltd
7th Floor, Infinity Tower C, DLF Cyber City,
Gurgaon 122 002, Haryana, India

Penguin
Random House
India

First published in Puffin Books by Penguin Random House India 2017

Text copyright © Raja Sen 2017
Illustrations copyright © Vishal K. Bharadwaj 2017

This is a work of fiction. Names, characters, places and incidents are either the
product of the author's imagination or are used fictitiously and any resemblance
to any actual person, living or dead, events or locales is entirely coincidental.

ISBN 9780143441311

Book layout by Neeraj Nath

Typeset in Garamond
Printed at Replika Press Pvt. Ltd, India

www.penguin.co.in

To my godchildren,
William & Dhaani.

This is personal.

Don was a man who loved to bake.
Oh, what desserts he would make.
The best in the land,
So good you'd kiss his hand
Just for a slice of his chocolate cake.

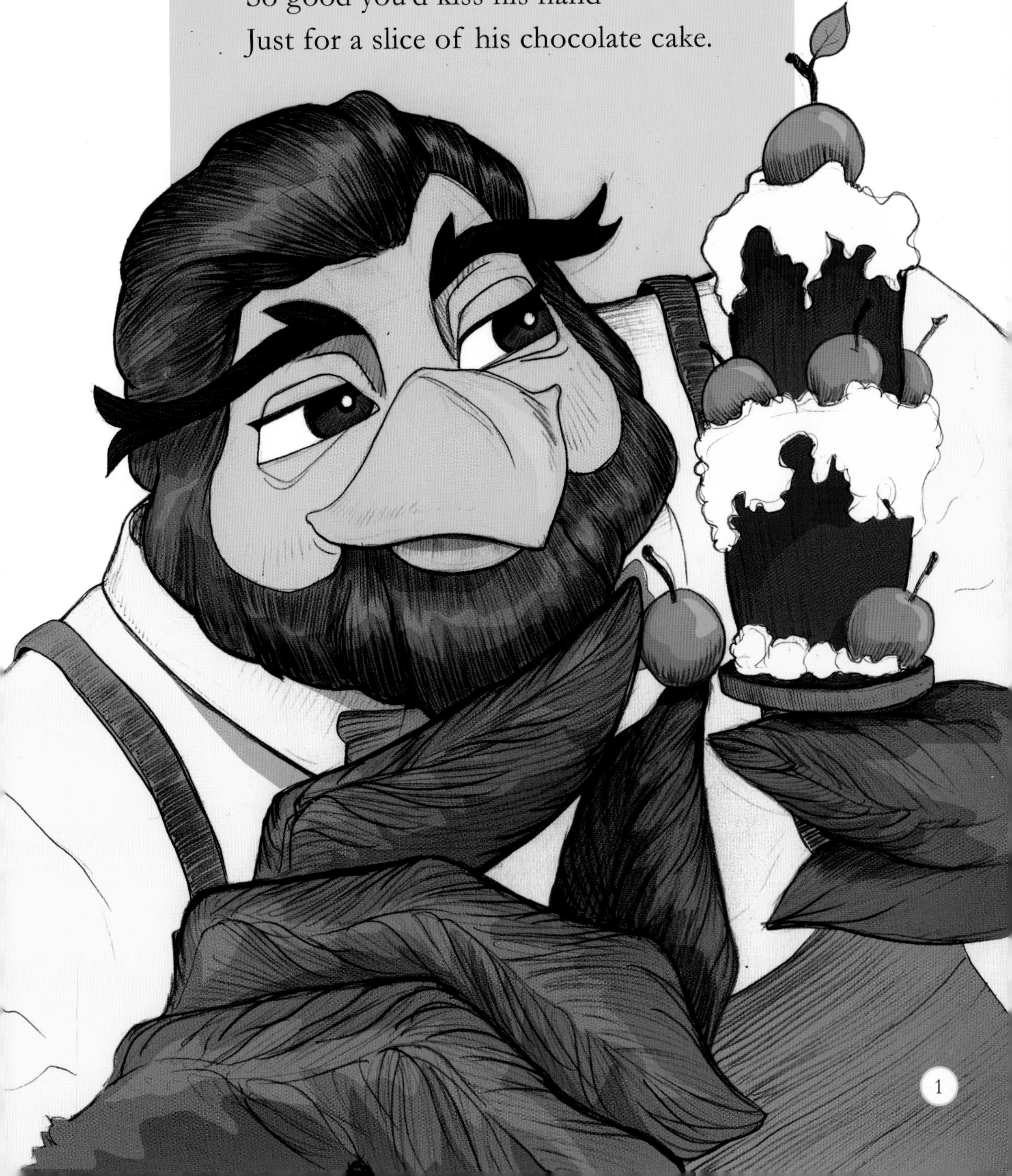

All the children would merrily peruse,
Taking so awfully long to choose:

Pastry or gobstopper?
So much was on offer.

There was no way
you could refuse.

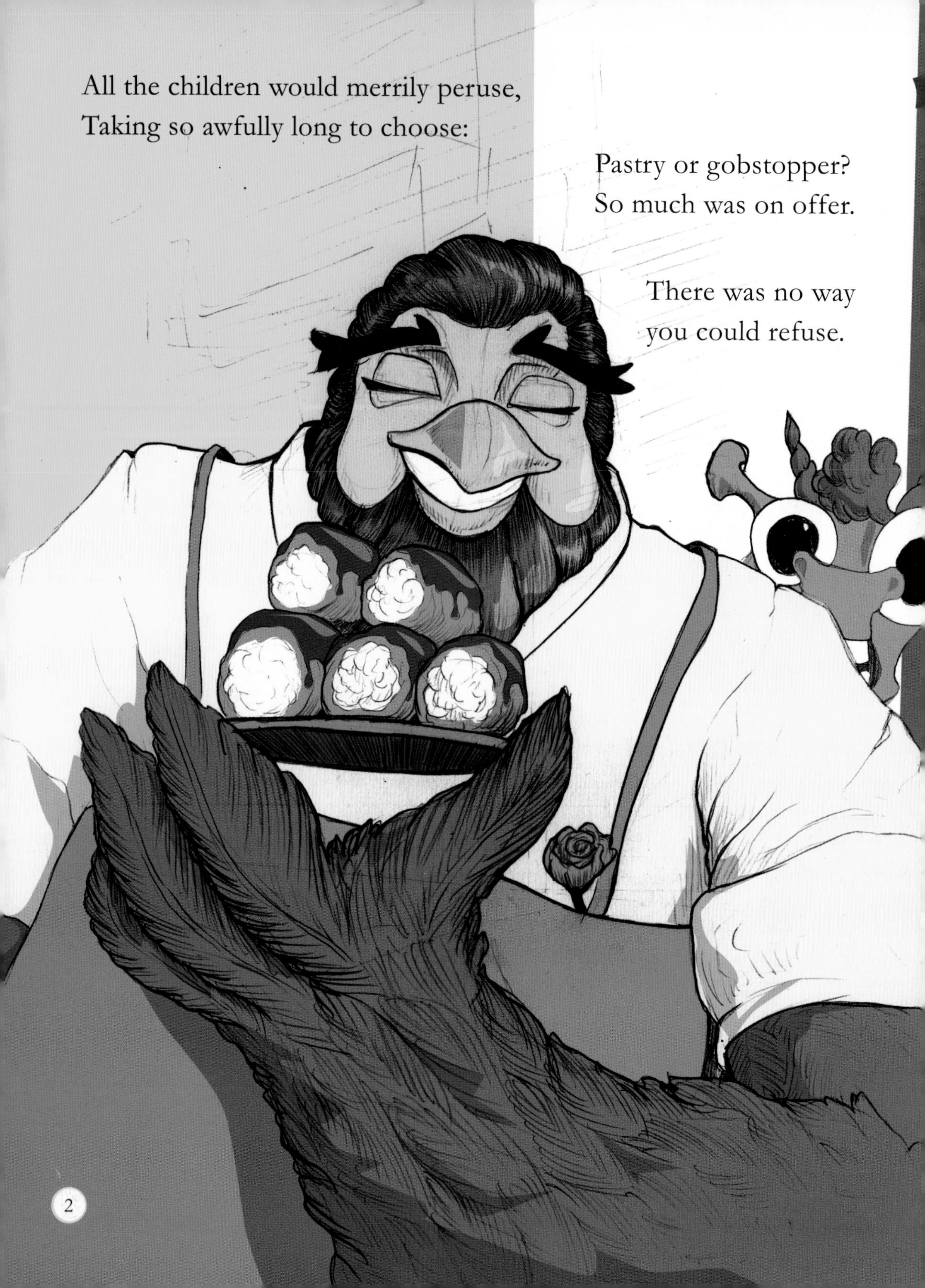

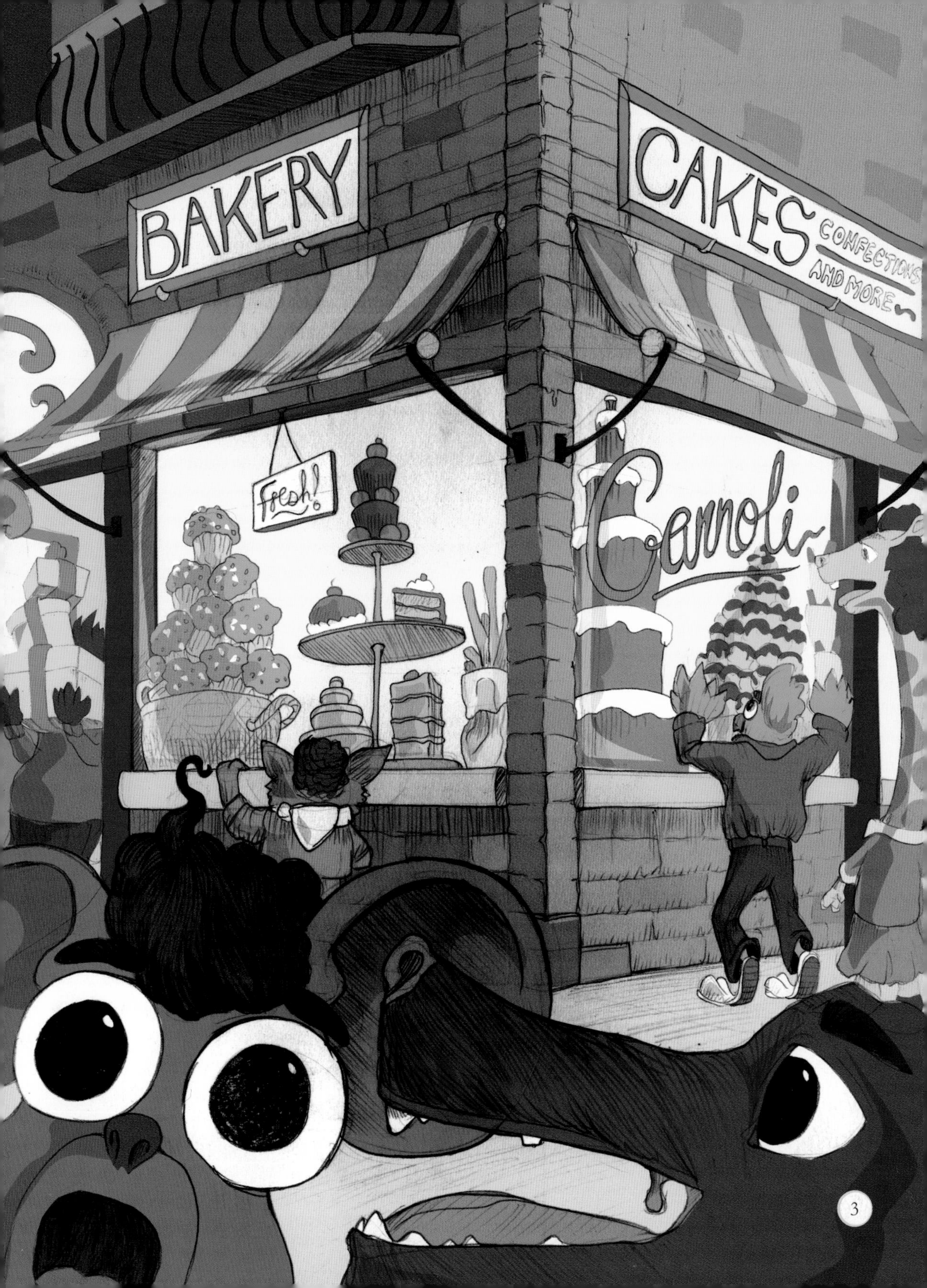
BAKERY
CAKES
CONFECTIONS AND MORE
Fresh!
Cannoli

It was his daughter Connie's birthday.
The kids were having a great time,
hooray!

Everyone loved the Don.
His parties went on and on,
And he practically
gave his cakes away.

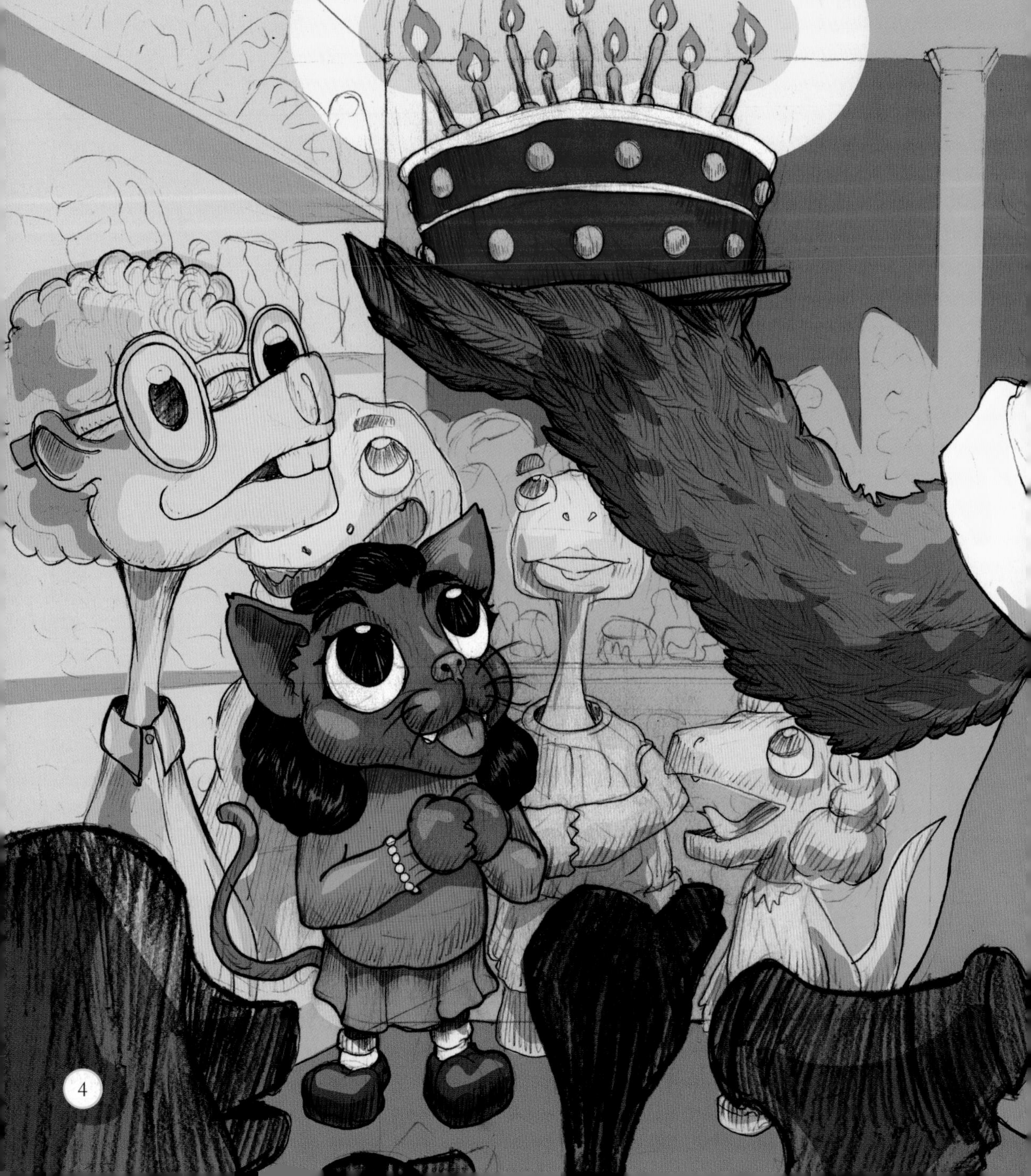

He made people smile with his sweets:
Eclairs, macaroons and so many treats.
Don gave them out for free.
He said, **'Just be nice to me.'**
Everyone bowed to him in the streets.

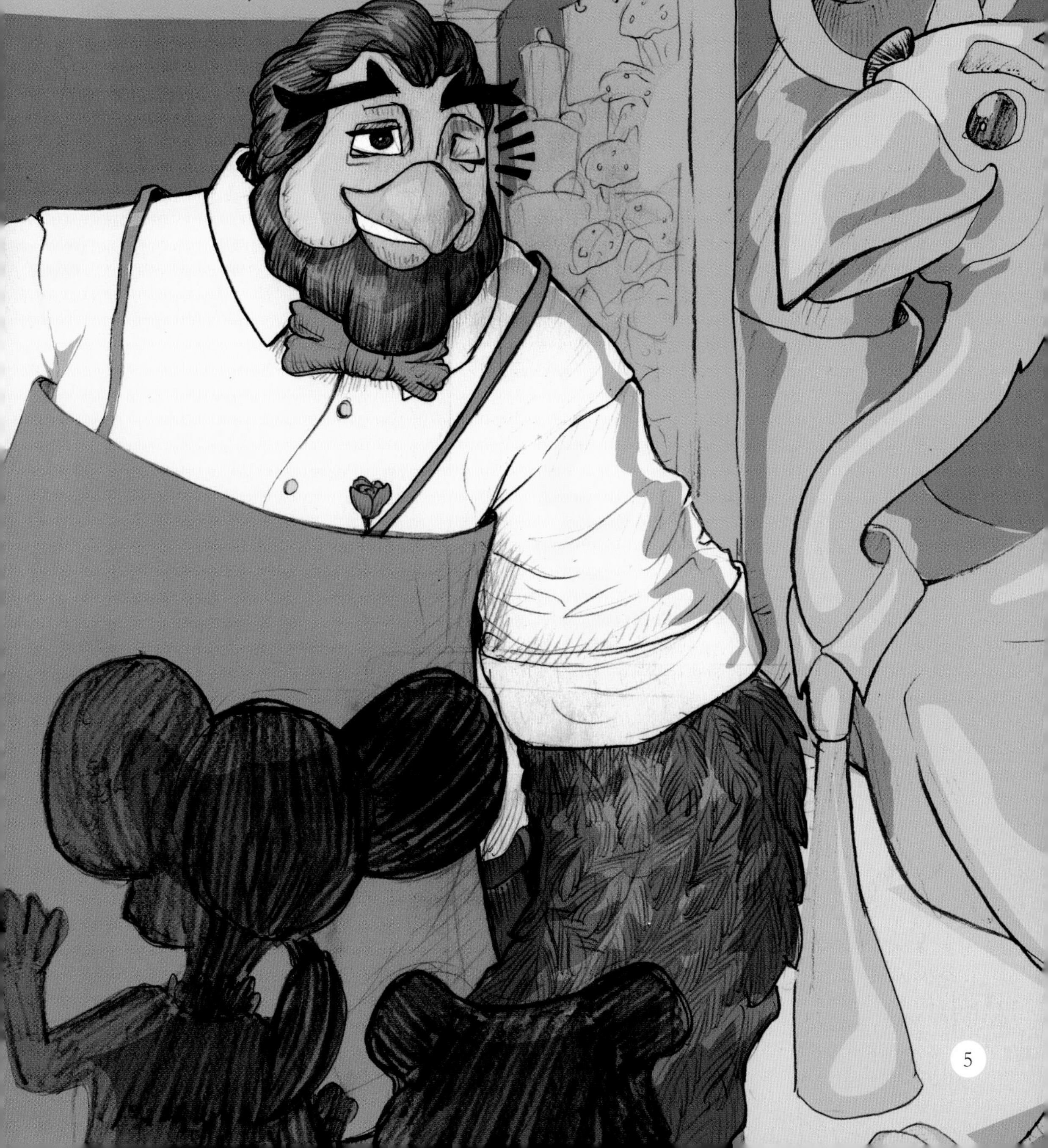

A rock star took the stage as the sun was sinking.
The kids gathered to hear Johnny Prince sing.

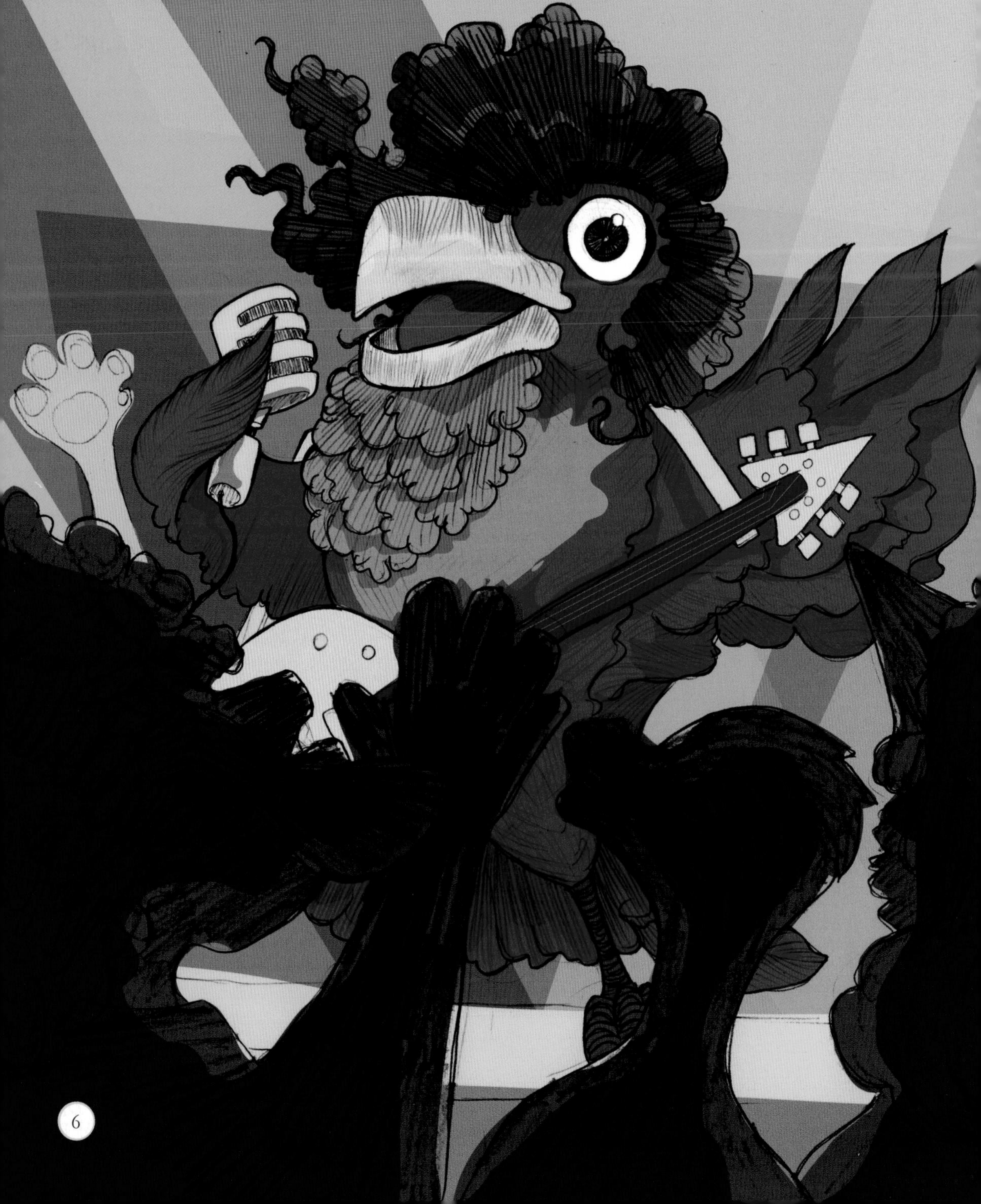

Yet a few little girls,
With an eye for curls,
Looked at Sonny in the back, doing his thing.

Sonny Cannoli was the Don's eldest child.
A boy with giant feet who ran wild.
He could be a bit rough,
Yet was charming enough.
Nobody could stay angry after he smiled.

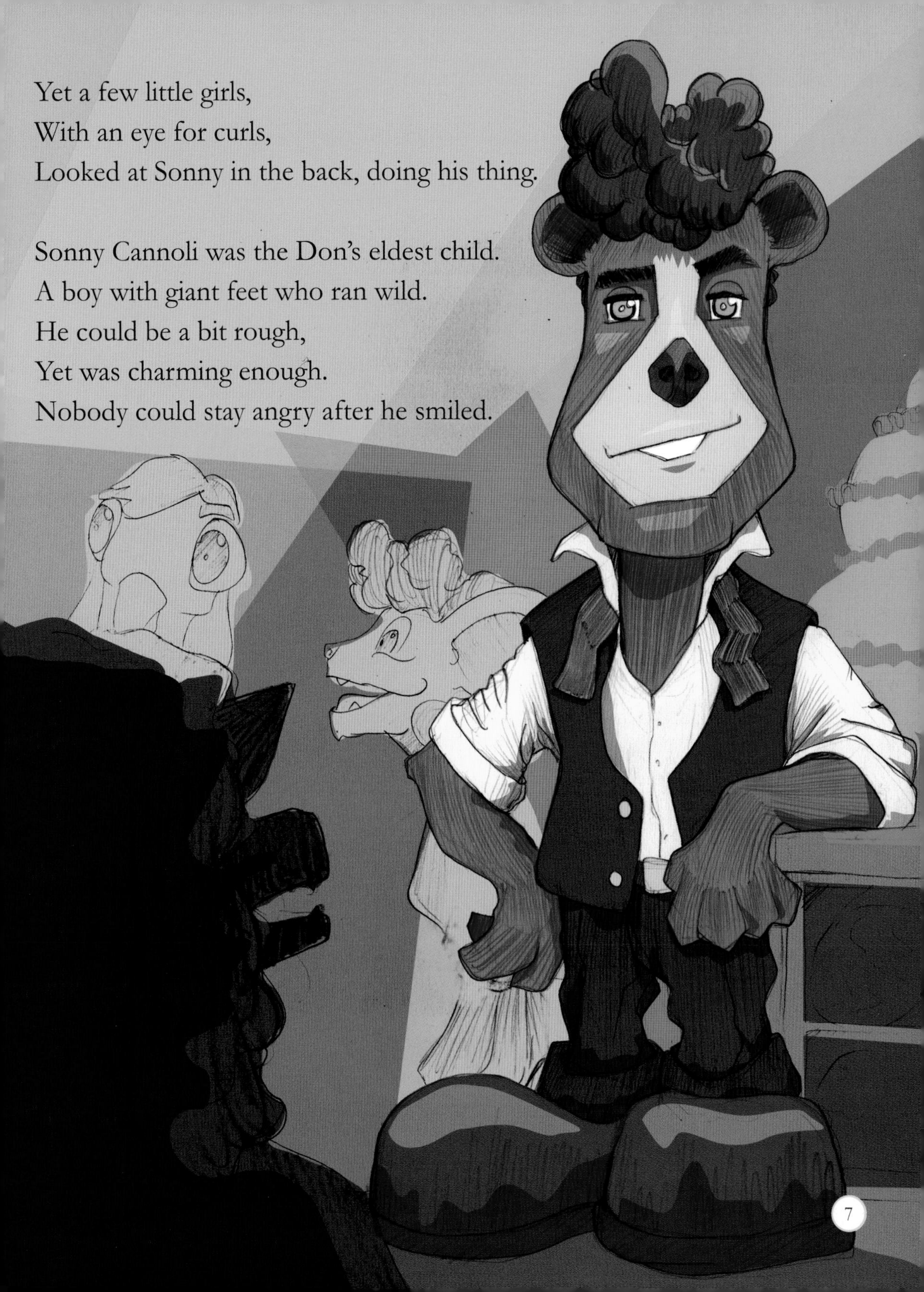

'Sonny is the eldest, then comes Freddo, then I,'
Said Michael to his friend Kay, with a sigh.
Michael was a bright spark,
Who liked his chocolate dark,
And wasn't really a bakery kind of guy.

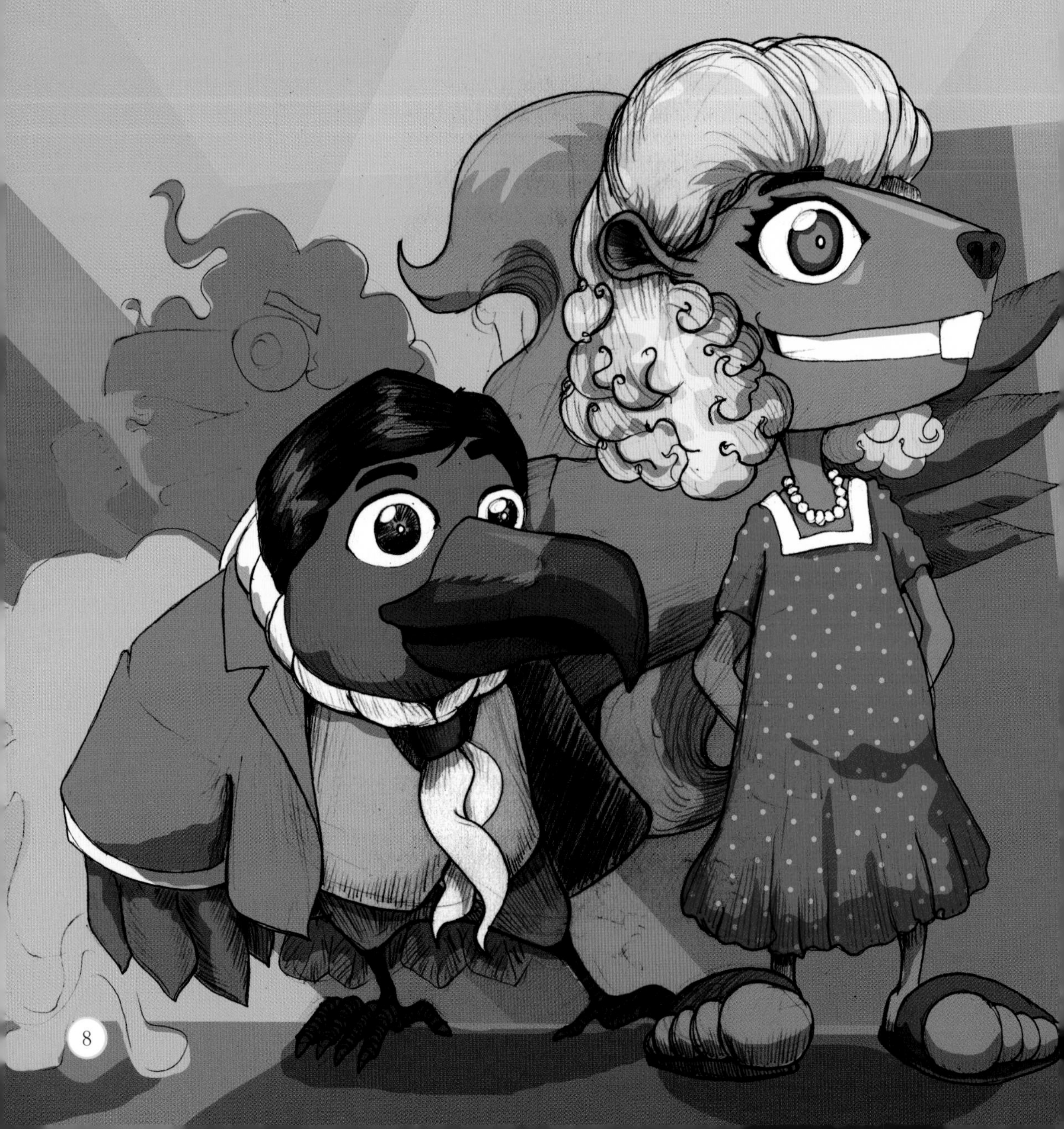

Freddo, the middle brother, was quiet and a bit silly.
Named after semifreddo: a dessert that shakes like jelly.
He came and smiled at Kay
In his simple, goofy way,
And she thought he was sweet (but also a little smelly).

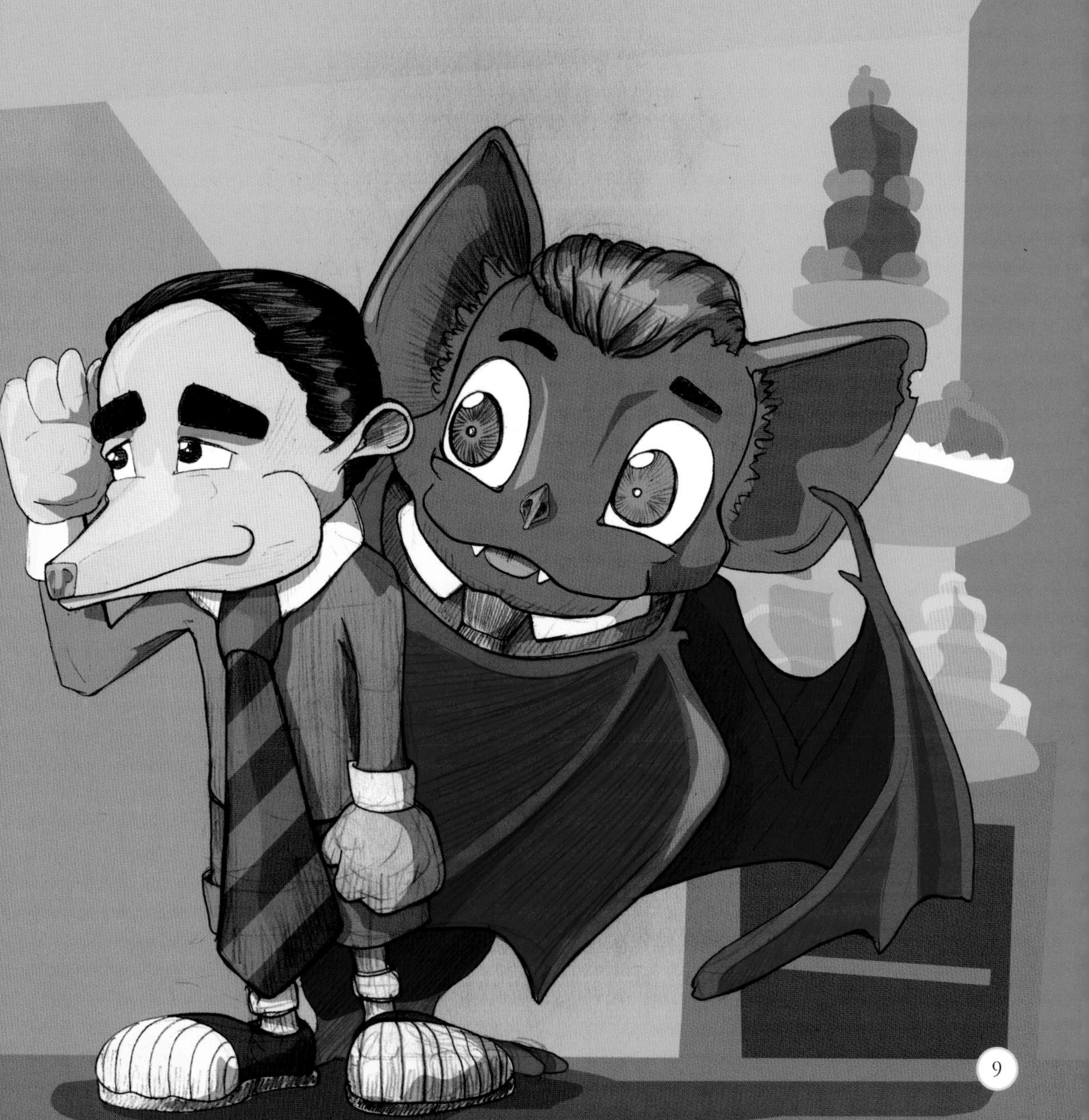

Michael told Kay how the Don helped Prince out
By frightening off a bully who would shout.
Jack would throw around his toys
And make the most irritating noise.
Michael's cousin Tom went to see what it was about.

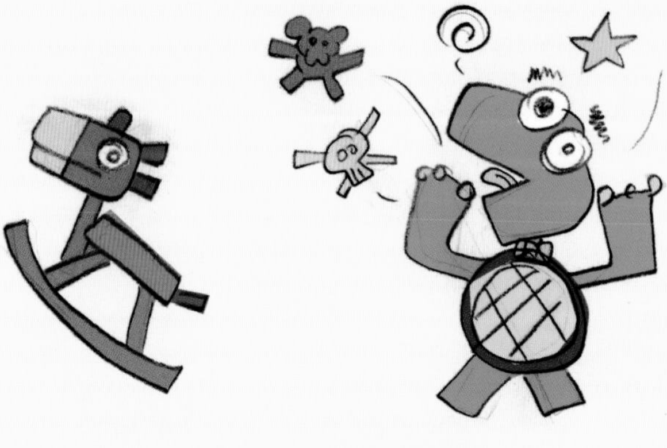

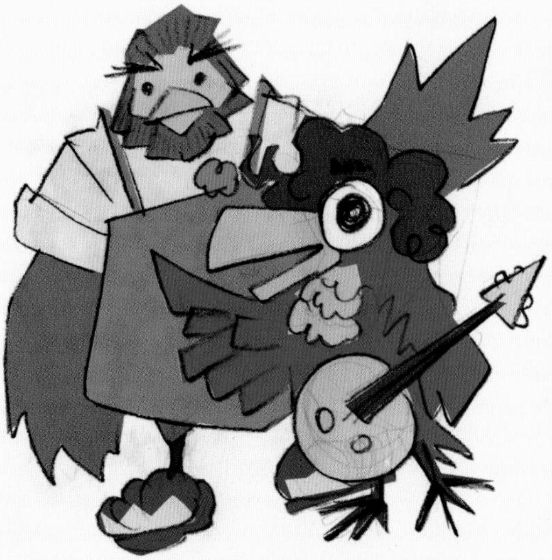

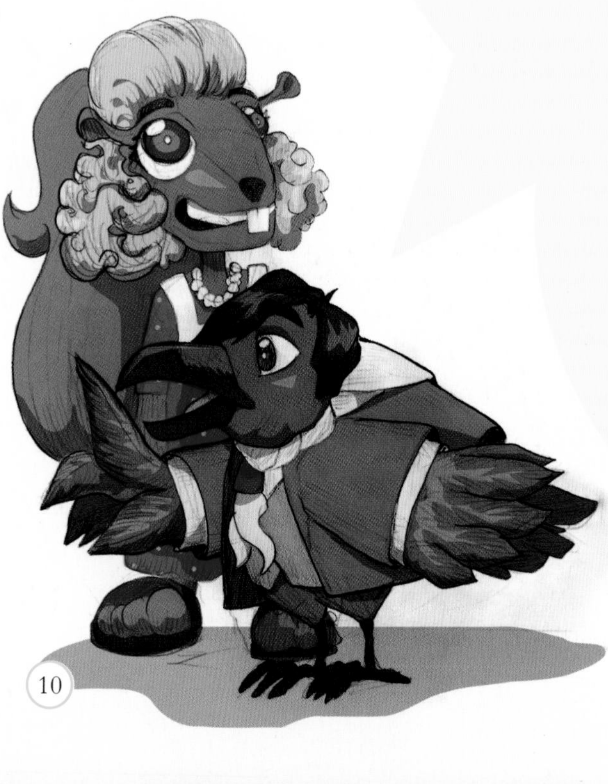

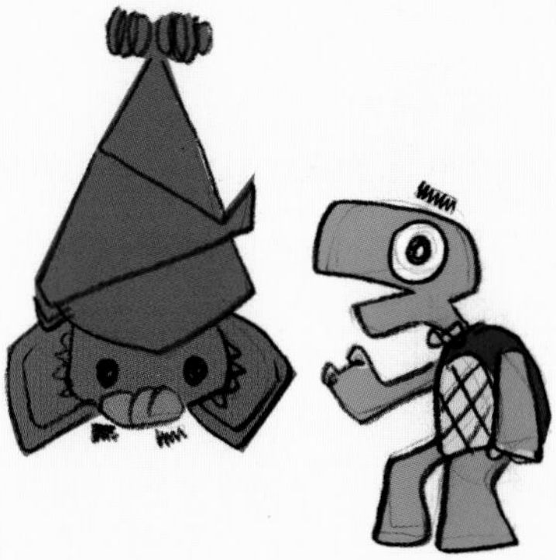

'I don't like that Johnny,' grumpy Jack said.
'His la-la-la singing makes me see red.'
Tom tried to explain,
It was all in vain.
So he dismantled Jack's rocking horse instead.

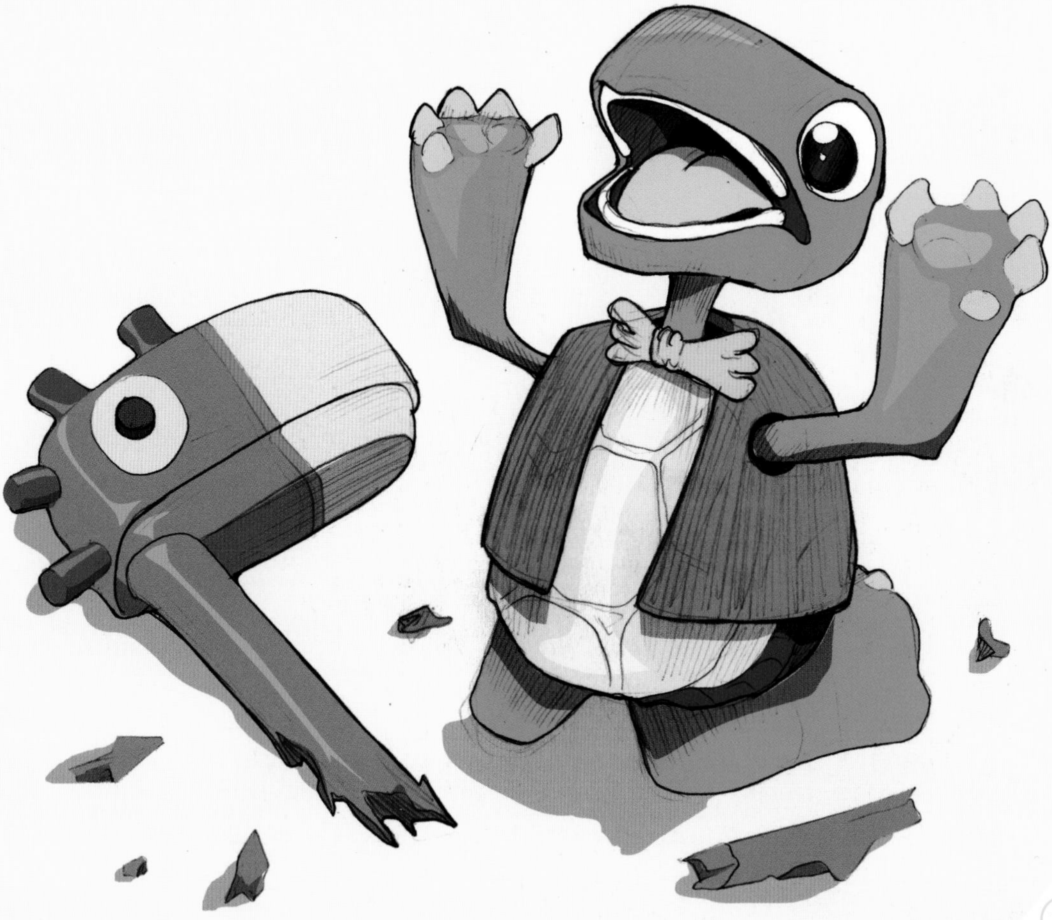

'This is my family, Kay, it's not me,'
Michael said, as she looked around to see
Big men practising their lines
So that their conversation shines,
And the Don would hand them a cake

or three.

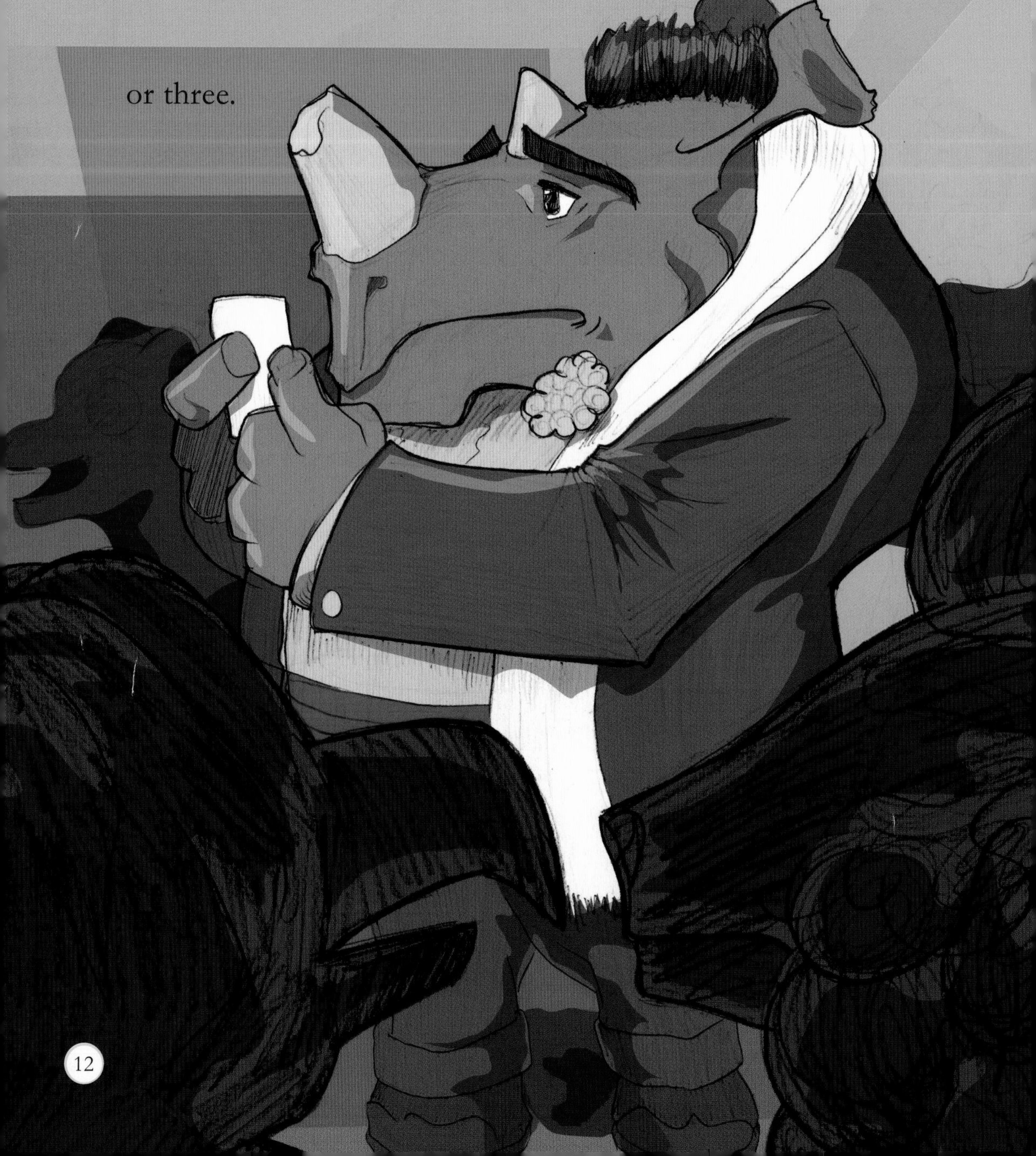

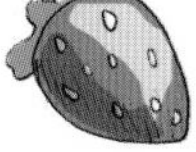

'It isn't important to cook,'
Michael demurred.

'So what if, on cheesecake, my family has the last word?

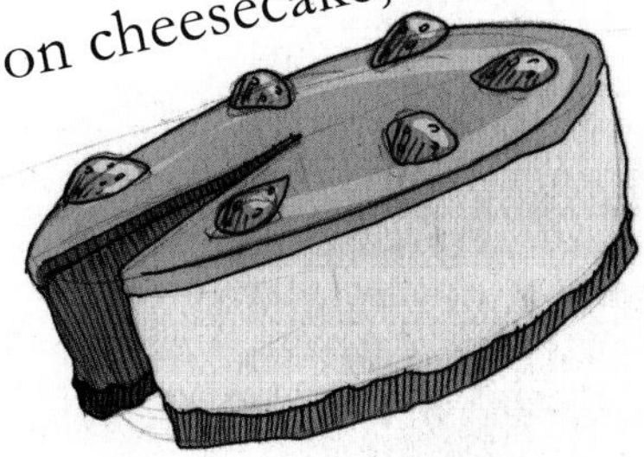

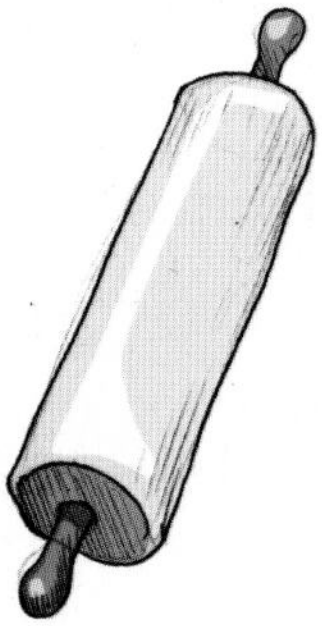

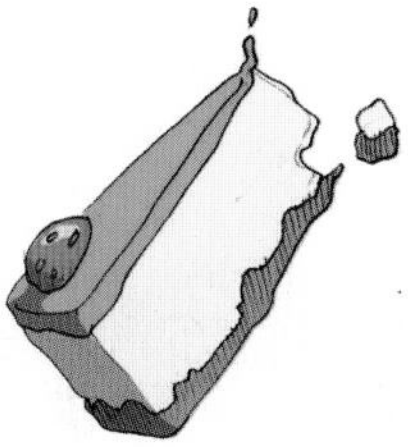

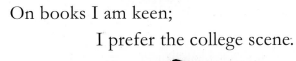

On books I am keen;
I prefer the college scene.

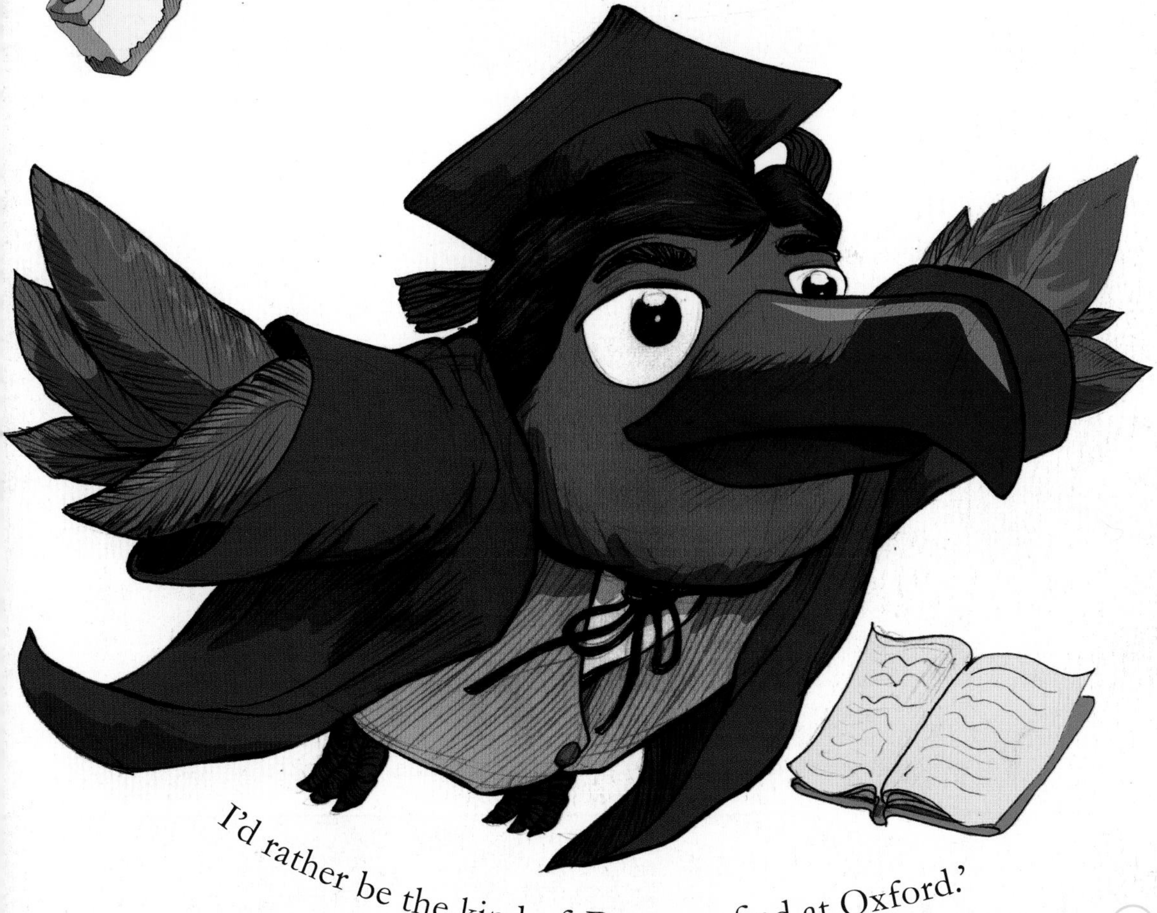

I'd rather be the kind of Don you find at Oxford.'

Finally, the Don danced with his girl.
He swept Connie up and gave her a twirl.
The whole family clapped;
Many a back was slapped.
All was indeed well with the world.

You see, it's all about the mouth.
To keep your mood from going south,
Flash a smile with ease,
Like you're saying 'cheese',
And eat something you

love,

when in doubt.

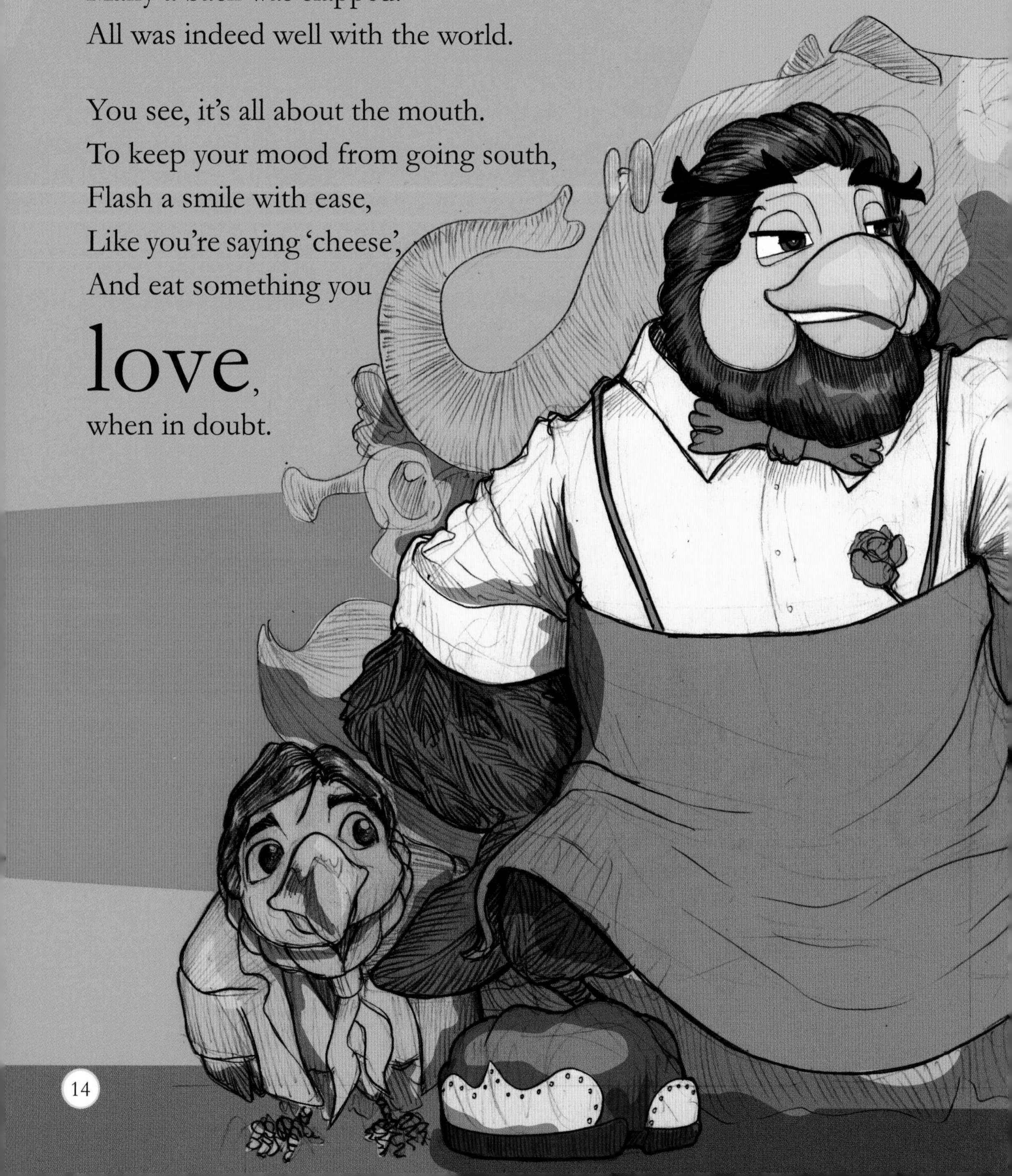

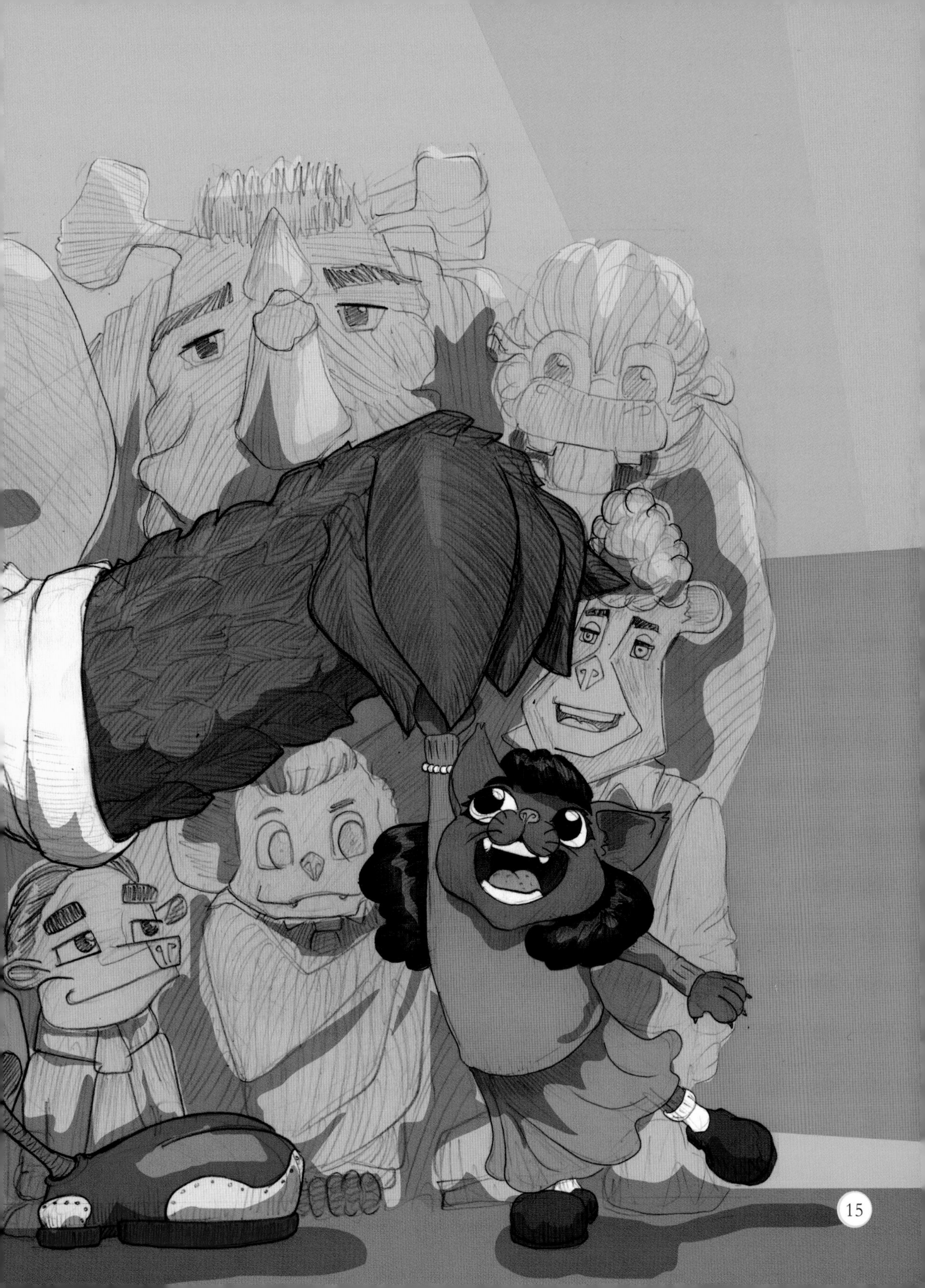

The next day, a shadow fell on the curtain.
Long-necked and twisted, it was certain
Mr Turk owned this shadow.
His stench was so bad, oh!
He made hard candies sold cheap, per ton.

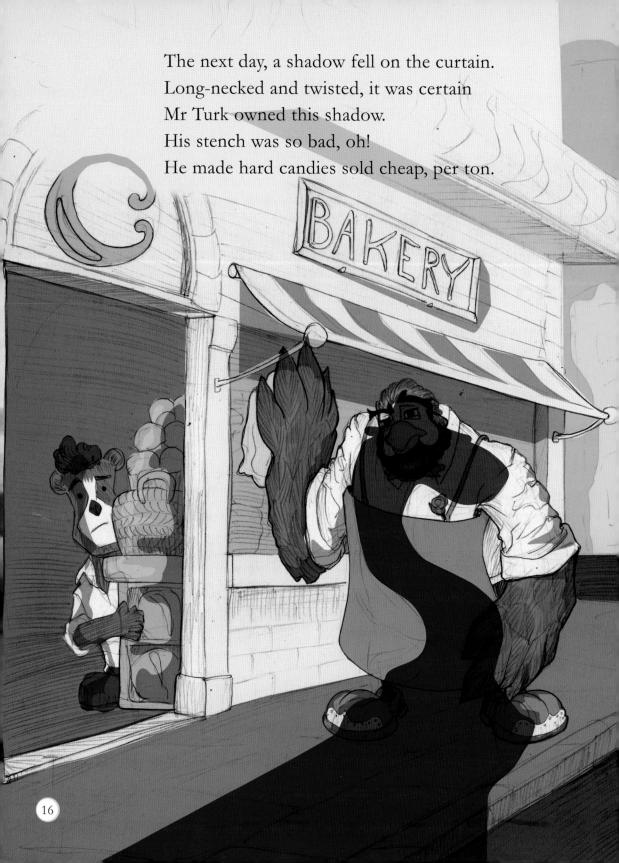

Turk showed Don his candies, trying his luck.
Sugary and round, harder than a hockey puck.
Big jawbreakers and lollipops
That could work as doorstops.
Sonny took one lick and went,

'Yee-uck!'

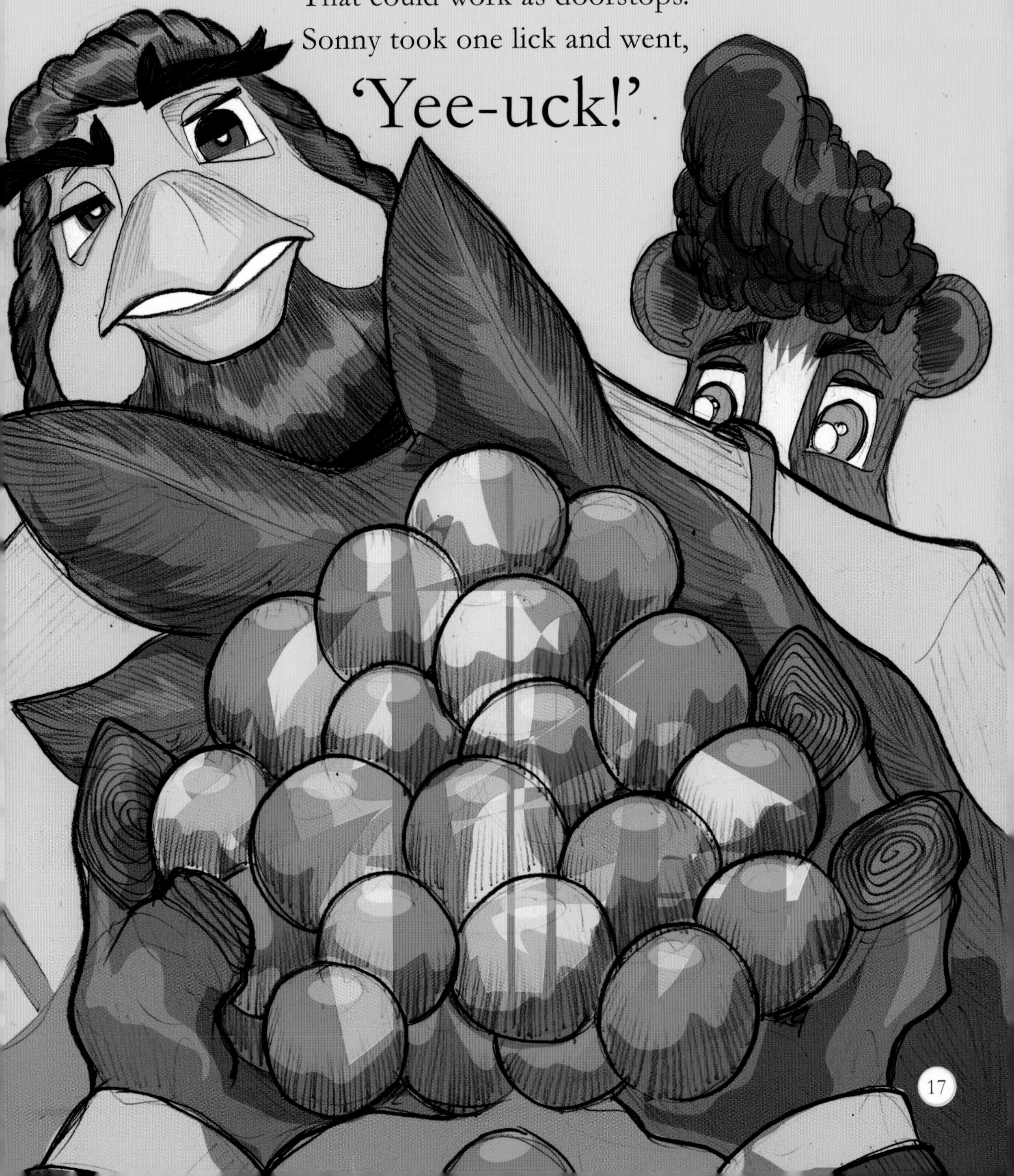

The Don shook his head slowly, side to side.
He said there was nothing at all here to decide.
So much sugar would make 'em sick.
Teeth would rot as kids ate quick.
They could choke if to swallow
they tried.

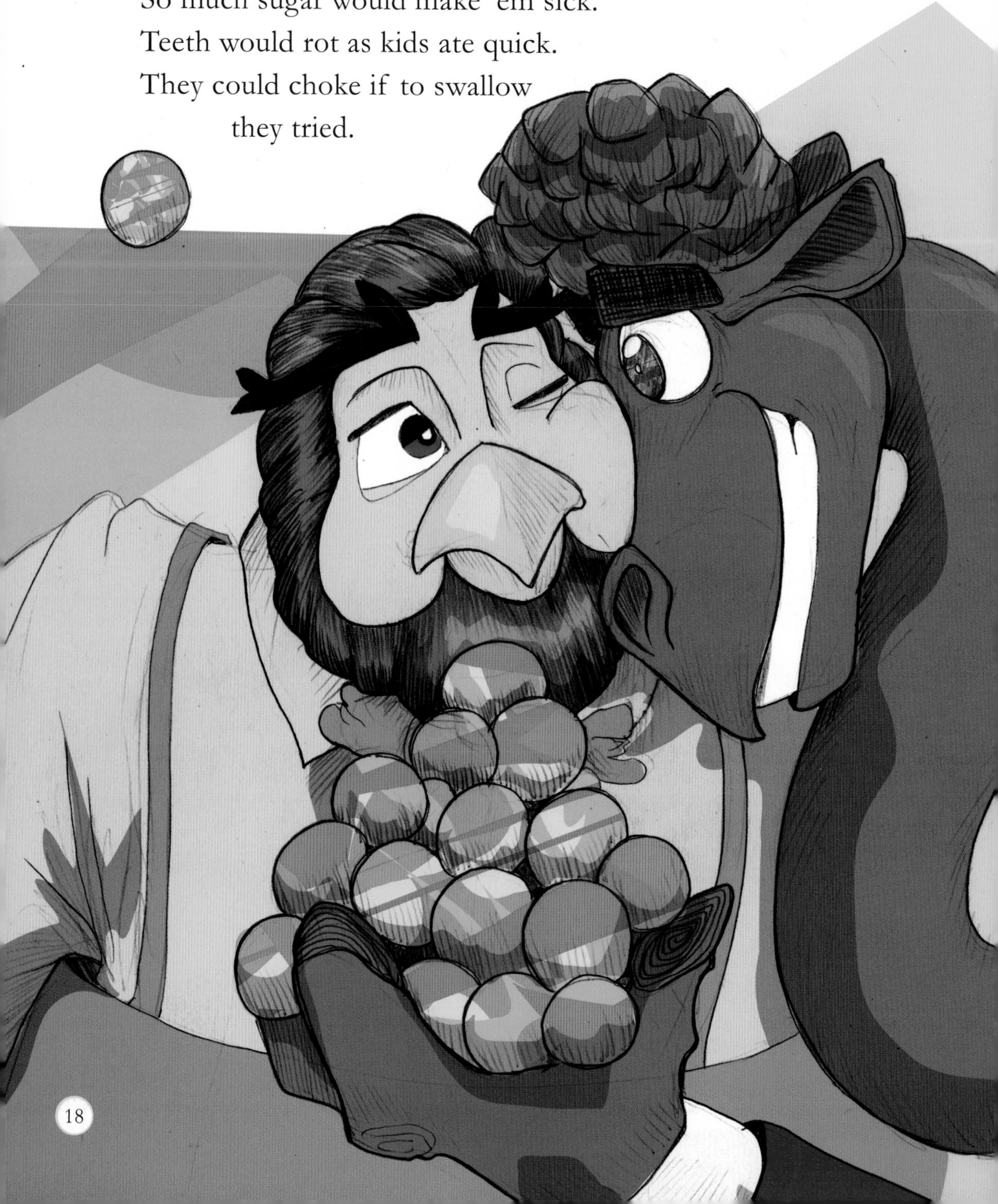

The Turk wanted the Don to help him sell.
He promised the candies would do so well.
They came in rainbow colours.
(What if they broke some molars?)
He guaranteed a hungry and eager clientele.

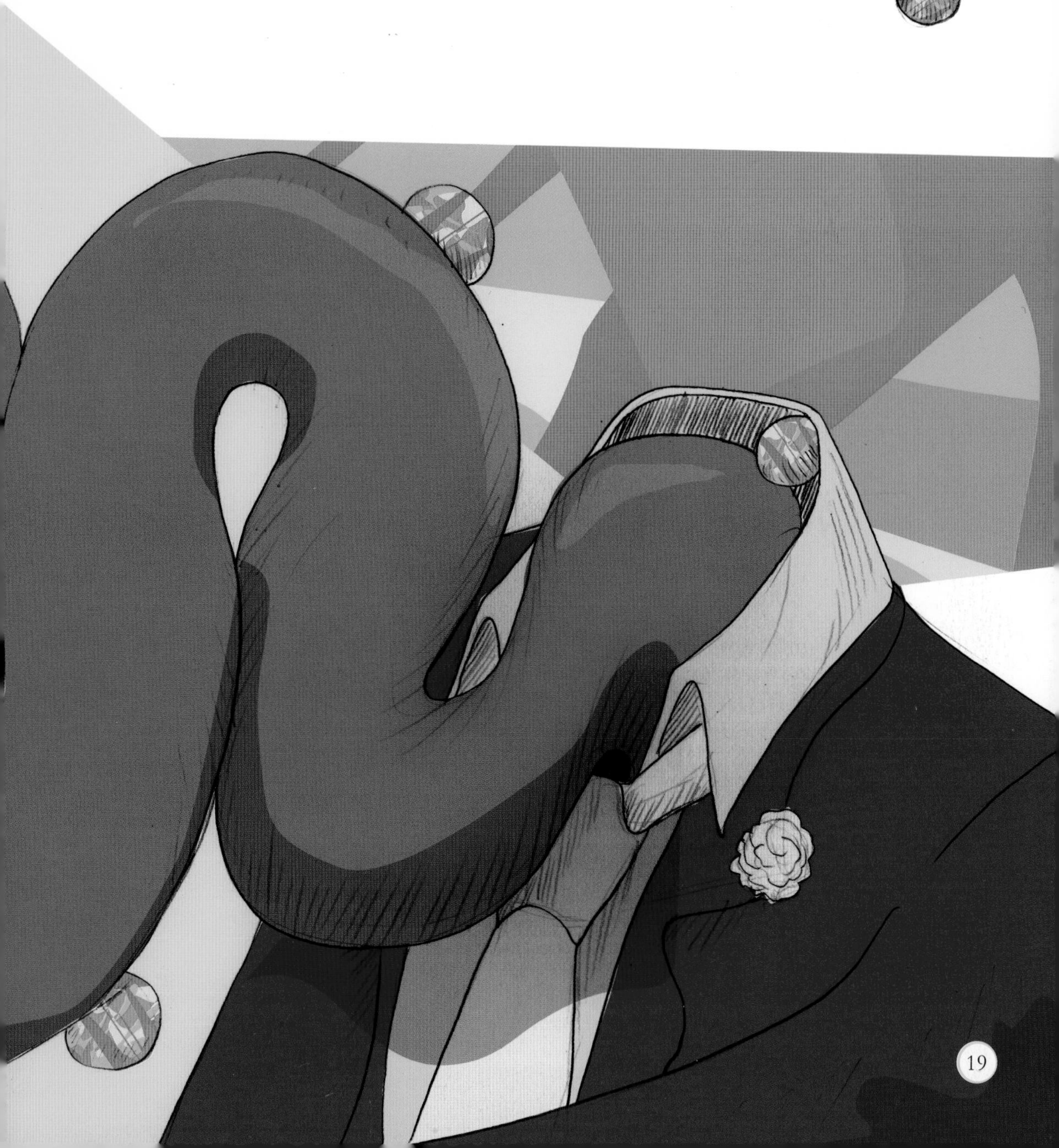

When the Don had made up his mind
There was no way to make him rewind.
So then Turk did scowl
And step out to growl,
For evil plans had to be designed.

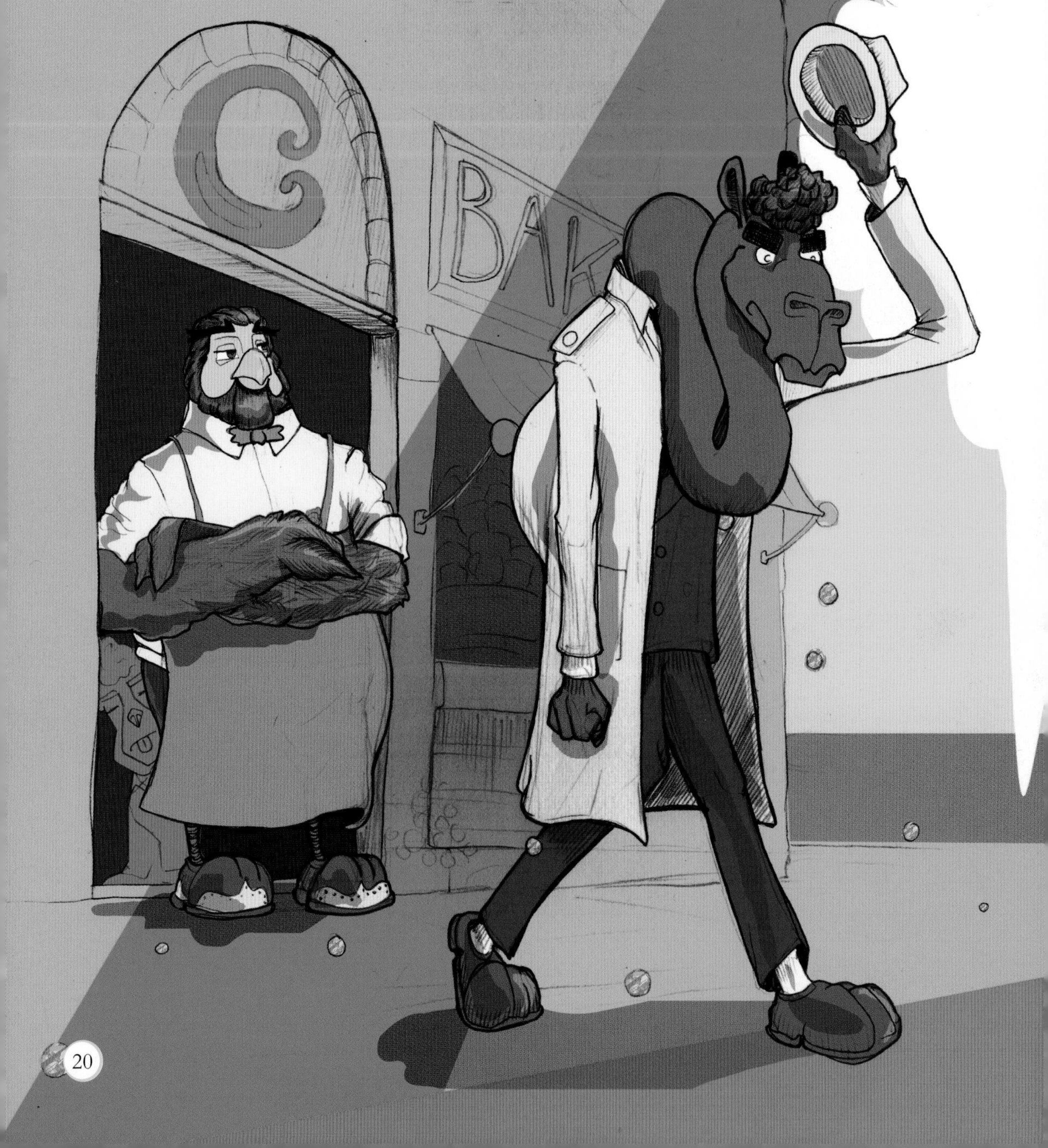

Turk rounded up bad bakers from all around,
Whose lemon tarts weren't fresh or very round.
The bullies came aboard,
Like Jack and his horde,

And little Henry who
on the hill
was found.

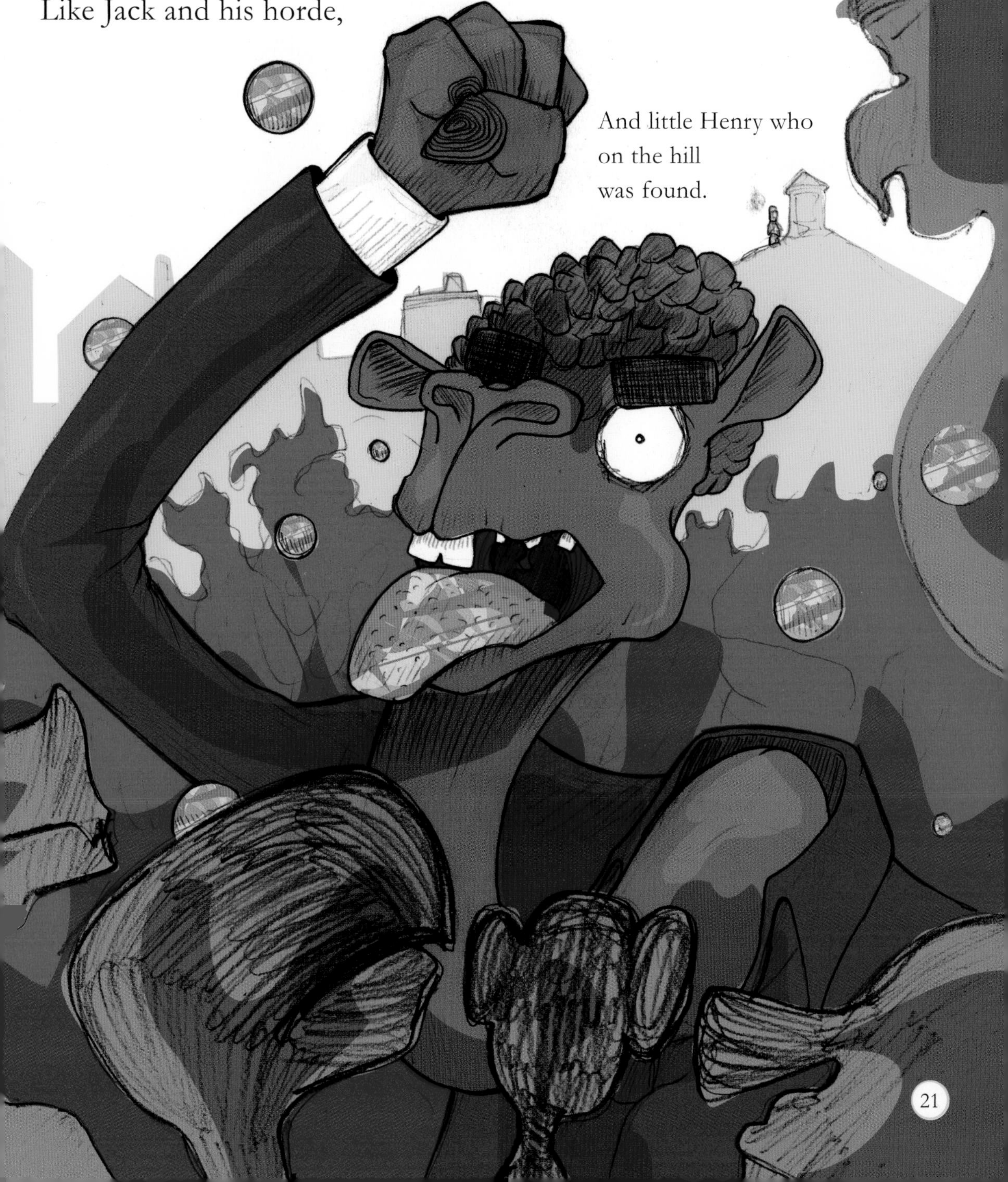

Because Michael liked his chocolate dark,
The Don decided, after a walk in the park,
To go buy some supplies
For the littlest of his guys
And make something that hits the mark.

If you want the very best dark chocolate cake,
Take cocoa, cream and a grown-up who can bake.
(It's easy, open sesame!
To help, here's the recipe.)
Note: Not having fresh oranges is a mistake.

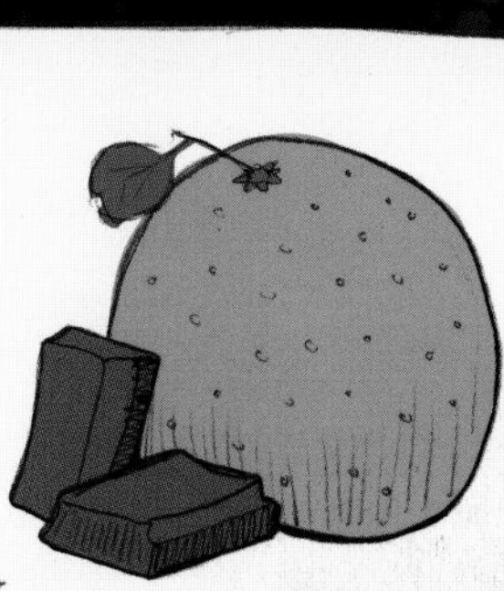

Chocolate Orange Cake

(MICHAEL'S FAVOURITE)

IN A SAUCEPAN, MELT 1/4 CUP SUGAR IN 1/4 CUP WATER, ADD IN 2 THINLY SLICED MANDARIN ORANGES & STEW UNTIL SOFT.

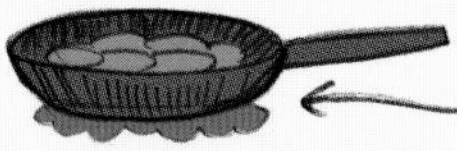

(low flame!)

MEANWHILE, COMBINE 1/2 CUP COARSE ALMOND MEAL, 1/2 CUP FLOUR, 1/4 CUP COCOA, 1/2 CUP SUGAR, 1/4 TSP SALT, 1 TSP BAKING POWDER, 1/4 TSP NUTMEG, 1/4 TSP CINNAMON, 1/2 CUP OF THE FINEST OLIVE OIL, 2 FRESH EGGS, AND A FEW SPOONS OF MILK AS NEEDED TO LOOSEN.

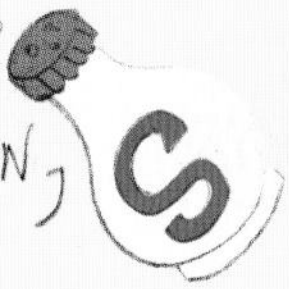

GREASE A CAKE TIN WITH A SPOON OF OLIVE OIL, THEN CAREFULLY ARRANGE THE STEWED ORANGE SLICES ON THE BOTTOM. (SNEAK IN A HALF CUP OF CHOPPED DARK CHOCOLATE. SHHHH!)

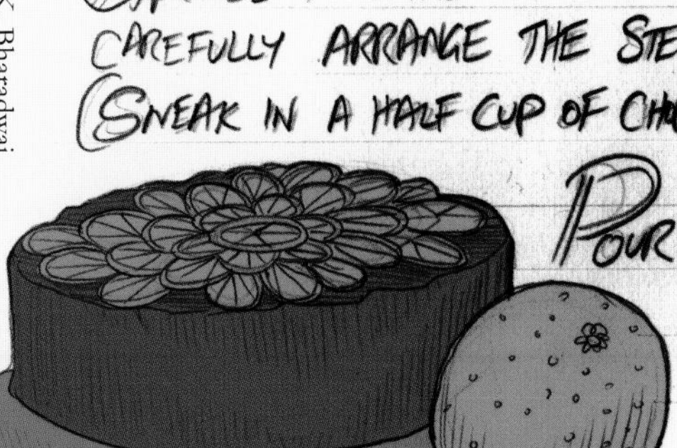

POUR IN THE BATTER & BAKE AT 180°C FOR 30 MINUTES (OR SO).

Eat Well!

Recipe co-developed by Swarupa Amin and Vishal K. Bharadwaj

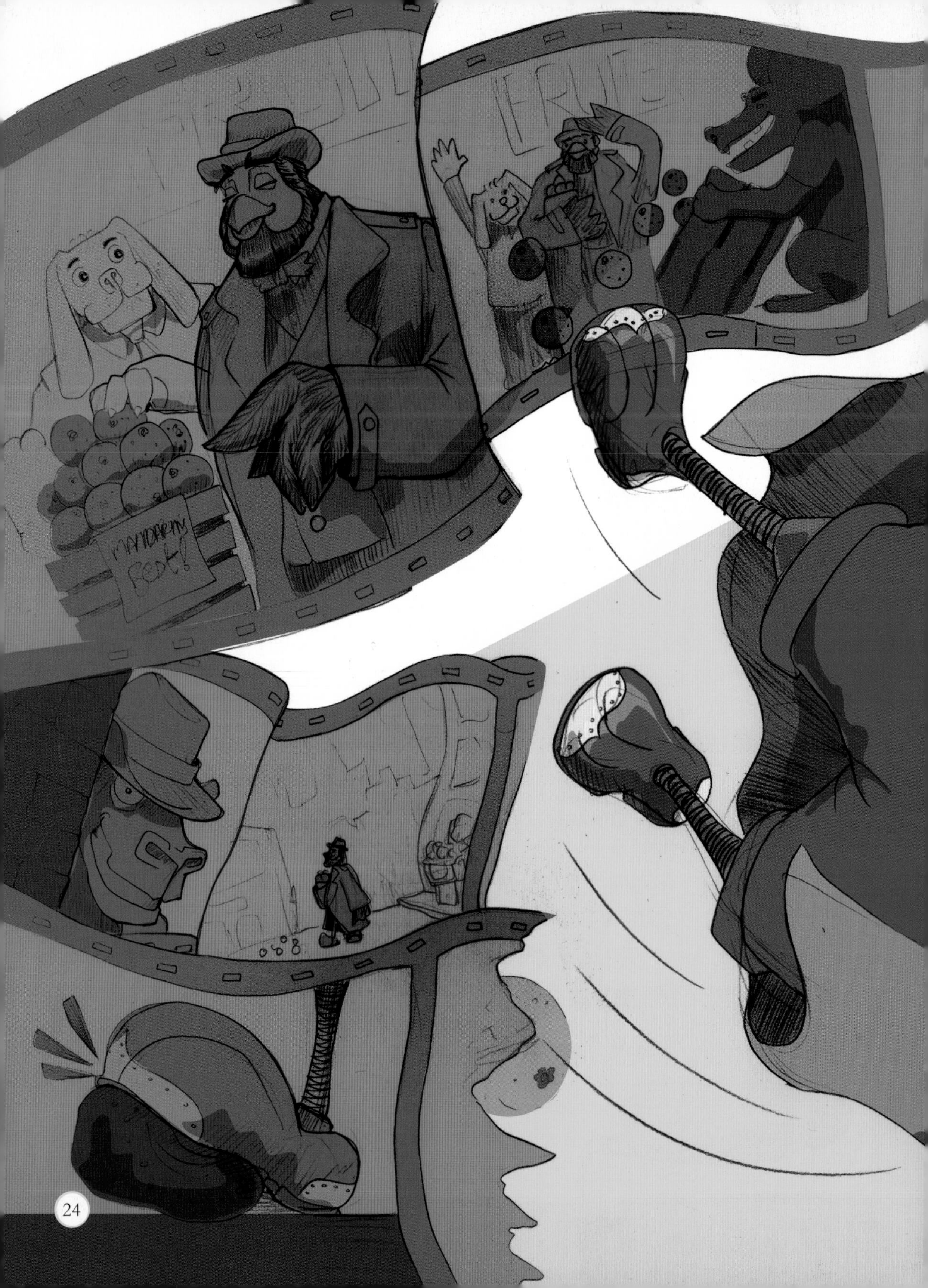
MANDARIN Fest!

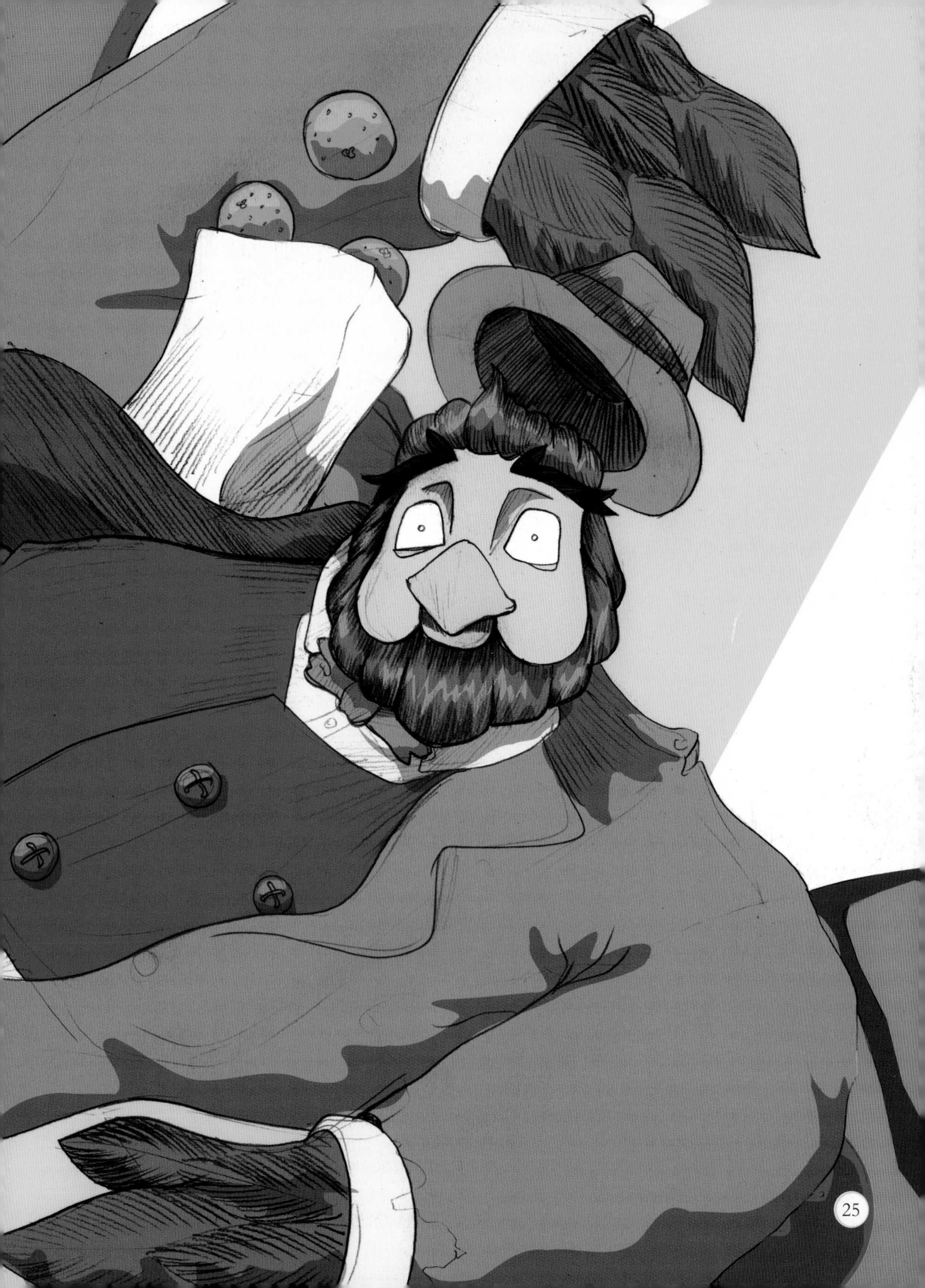

'Twas thus on oranges that the Don slipped.
Even as he fell, his bag he tightly gripped.
Helplessly Freddo fumbled,
Watching his dad stumble.
The entire neighbourhood's morale dipped.

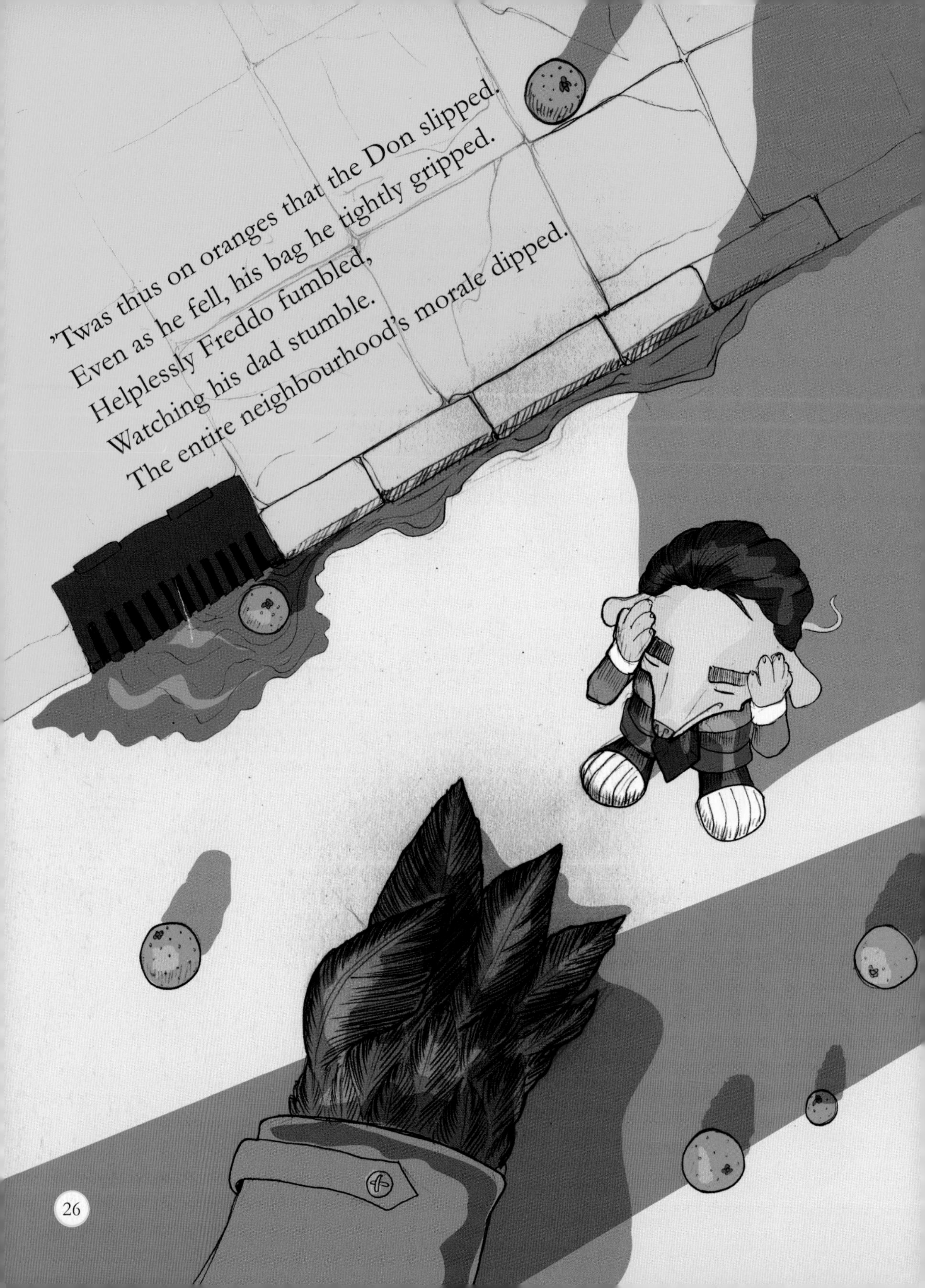

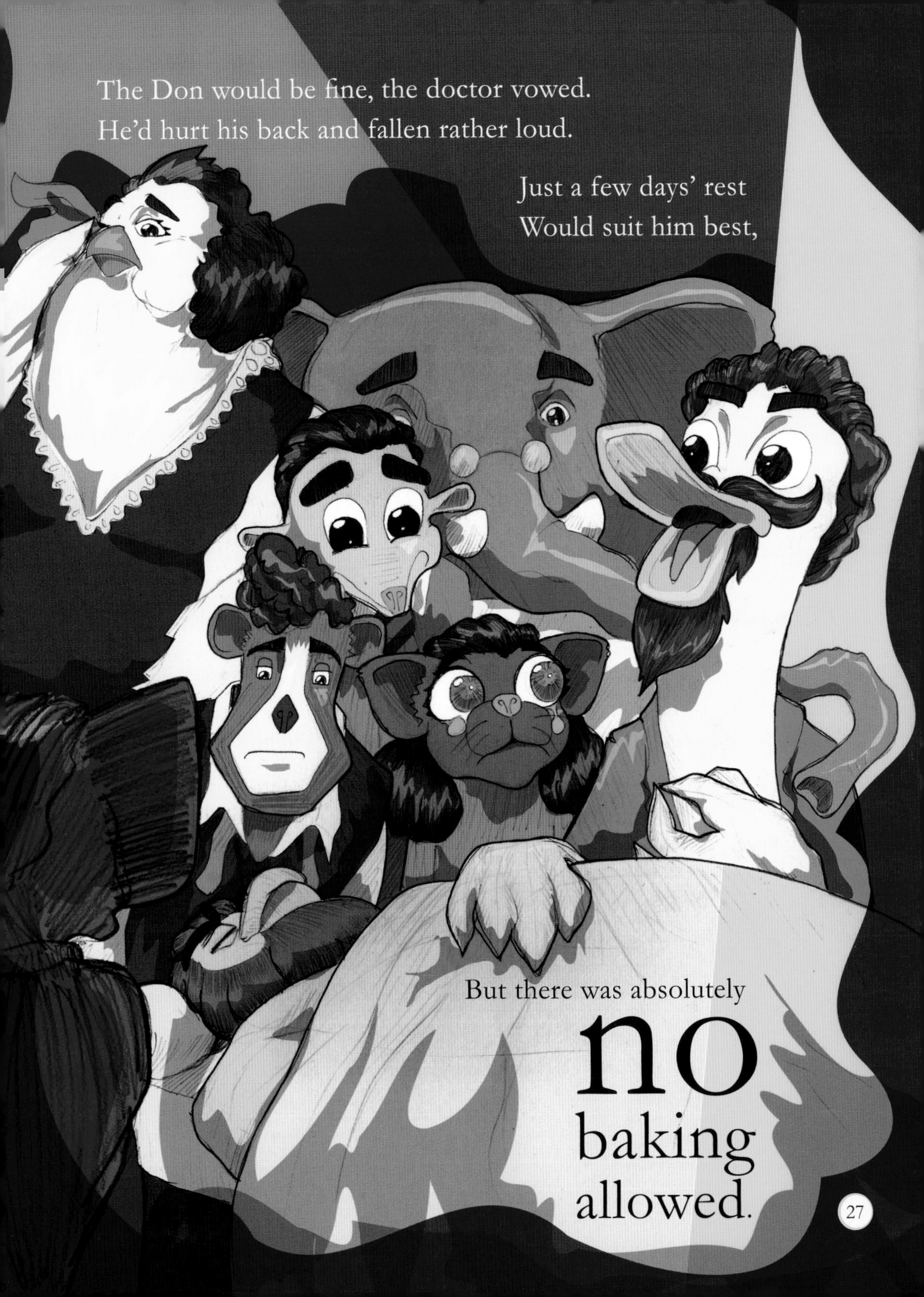

The Don would be fine, the doctor vowed.
He'd hurt his back and fallen rather loud.

Just a few days' rest
Would suit him best,

But there was absolutely

no
baking
allowed.

'Would you like me better if I were a car?'
Kay playfully asked the question bizarre.
Michael shook his head no;
They smiled together so,
Walking out of the latest movie from Pixar.

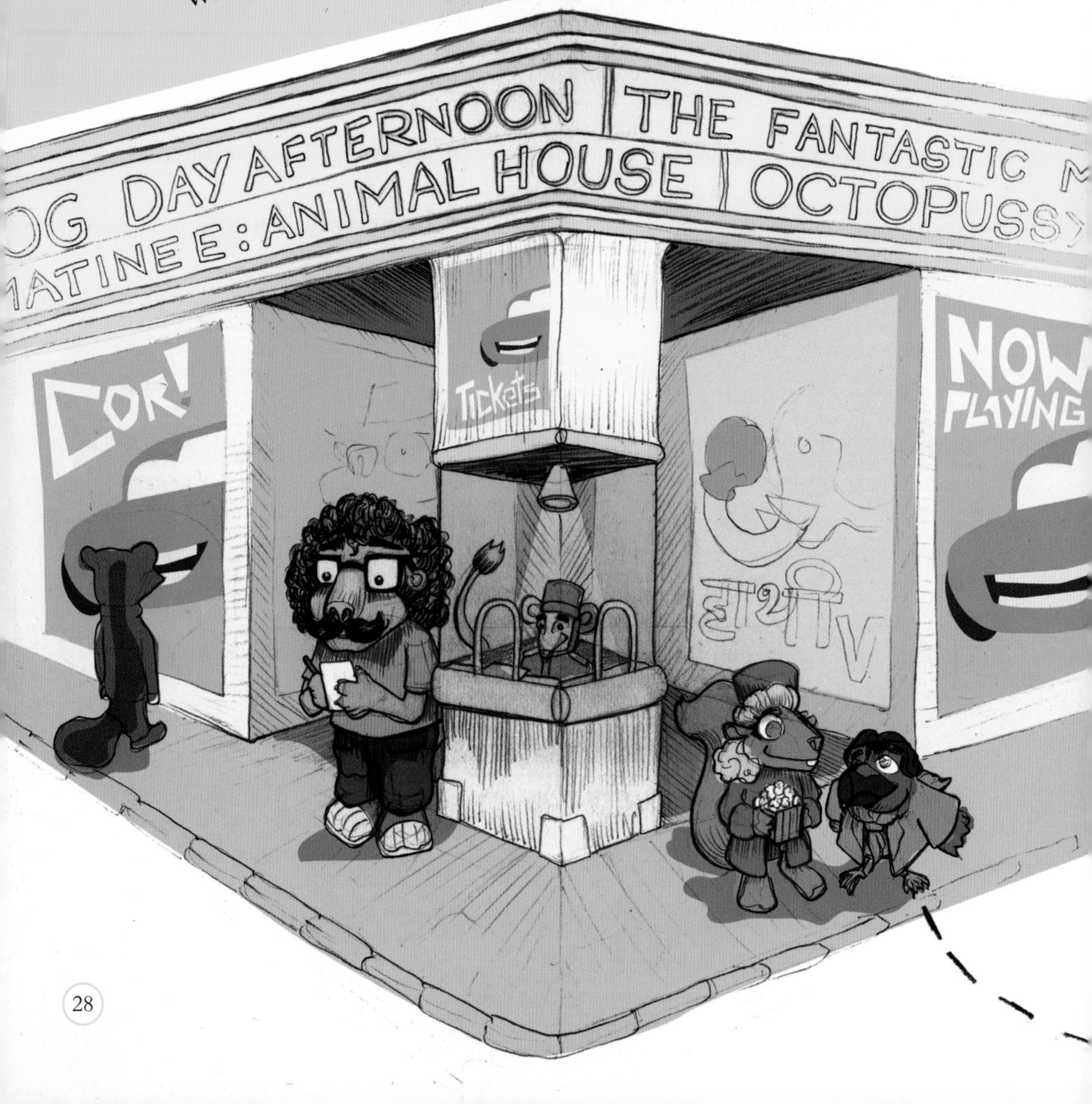
OG DAY AFTERNOON | THE FANTASTIC M
MATINEE: ANIMAL HOUSE | OCTOPUSSY
COR!
Tickets
NOW PLAYING

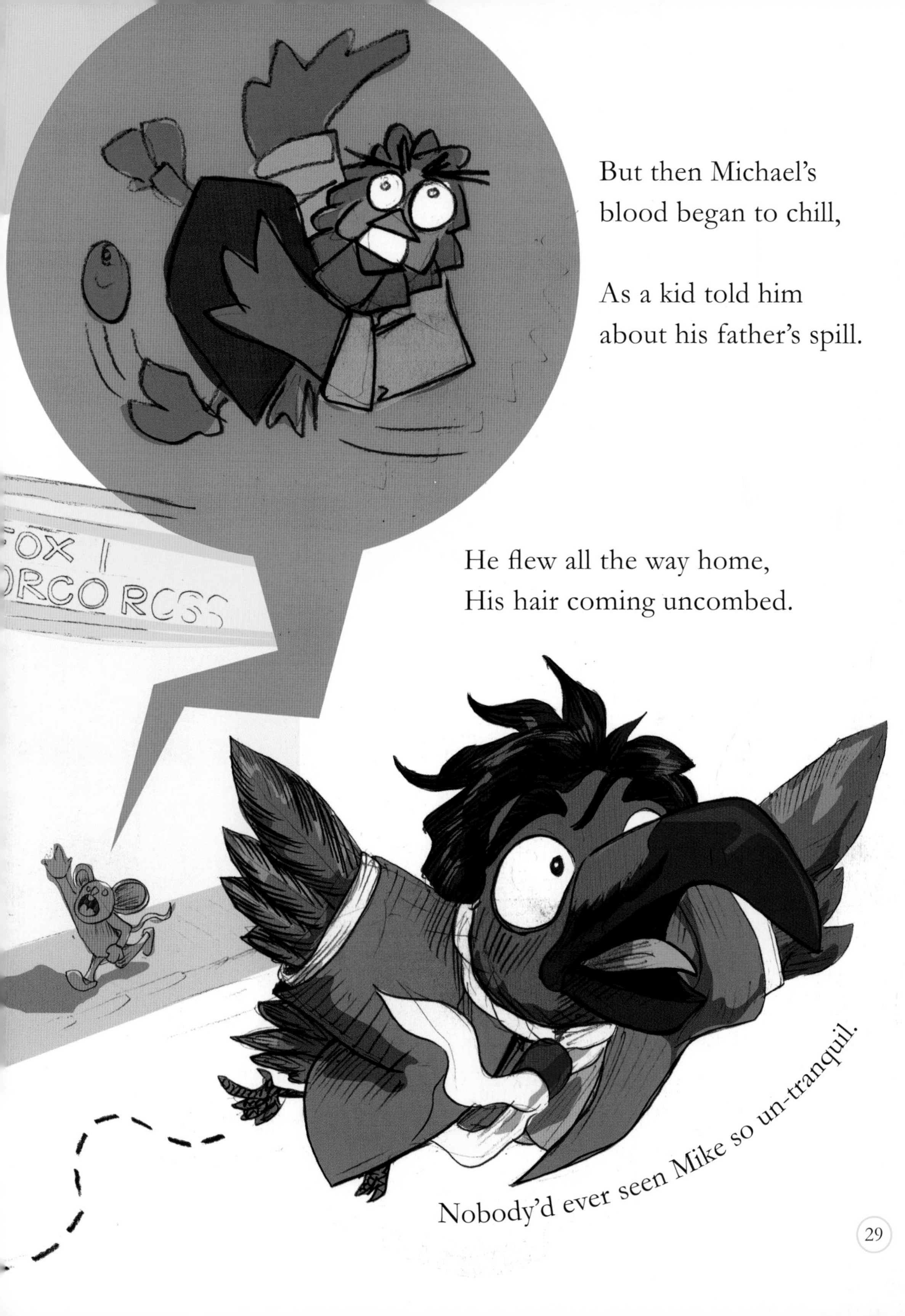

But then Michael's
blood began to chill,

As a kid told him
about his father's spill.

He flew all the way home,
His hair coming uncombed.

Nobody'd ever seen Mike so un-tranquil.

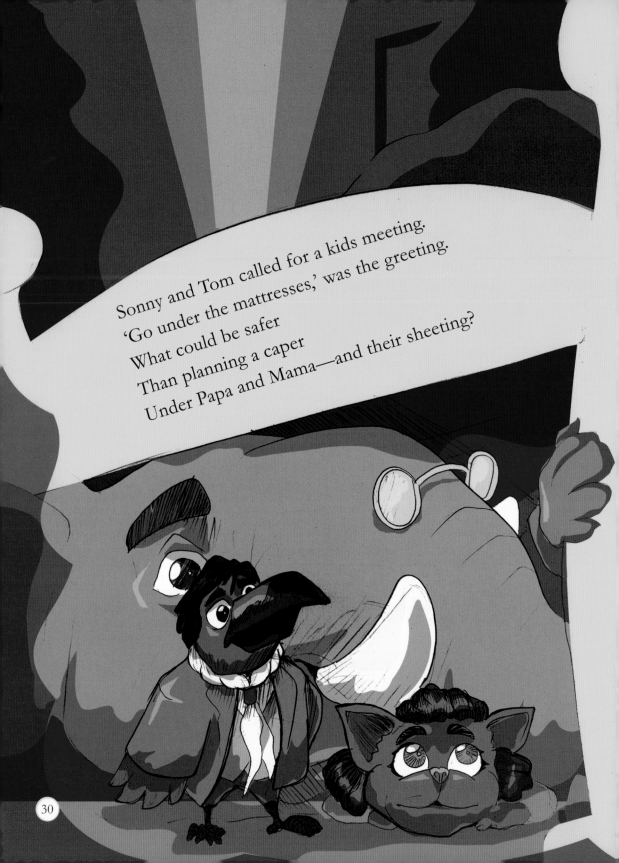

Sonny and Tom called for a kids meeting.
'Go under the mattresses,' was the greeting.
What could be safer
Than planning a caper
Under Papa and Mama—and their sheeting?

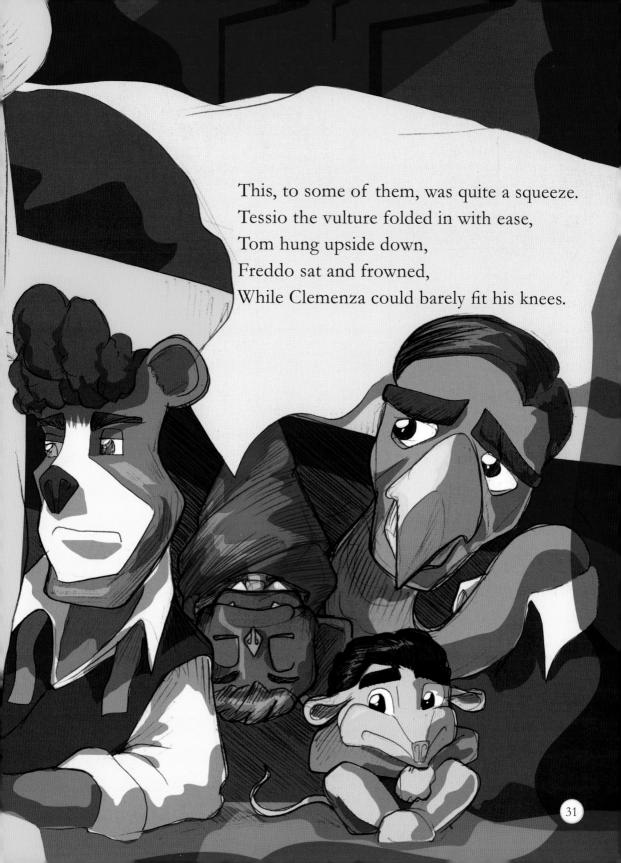

This, to some of them, was quite a squeeze.
Tessio the vulture folded in with ease,
Tom hung upside down,
Freddo sat and frowned,
While Clemenza could barely fit his knees.

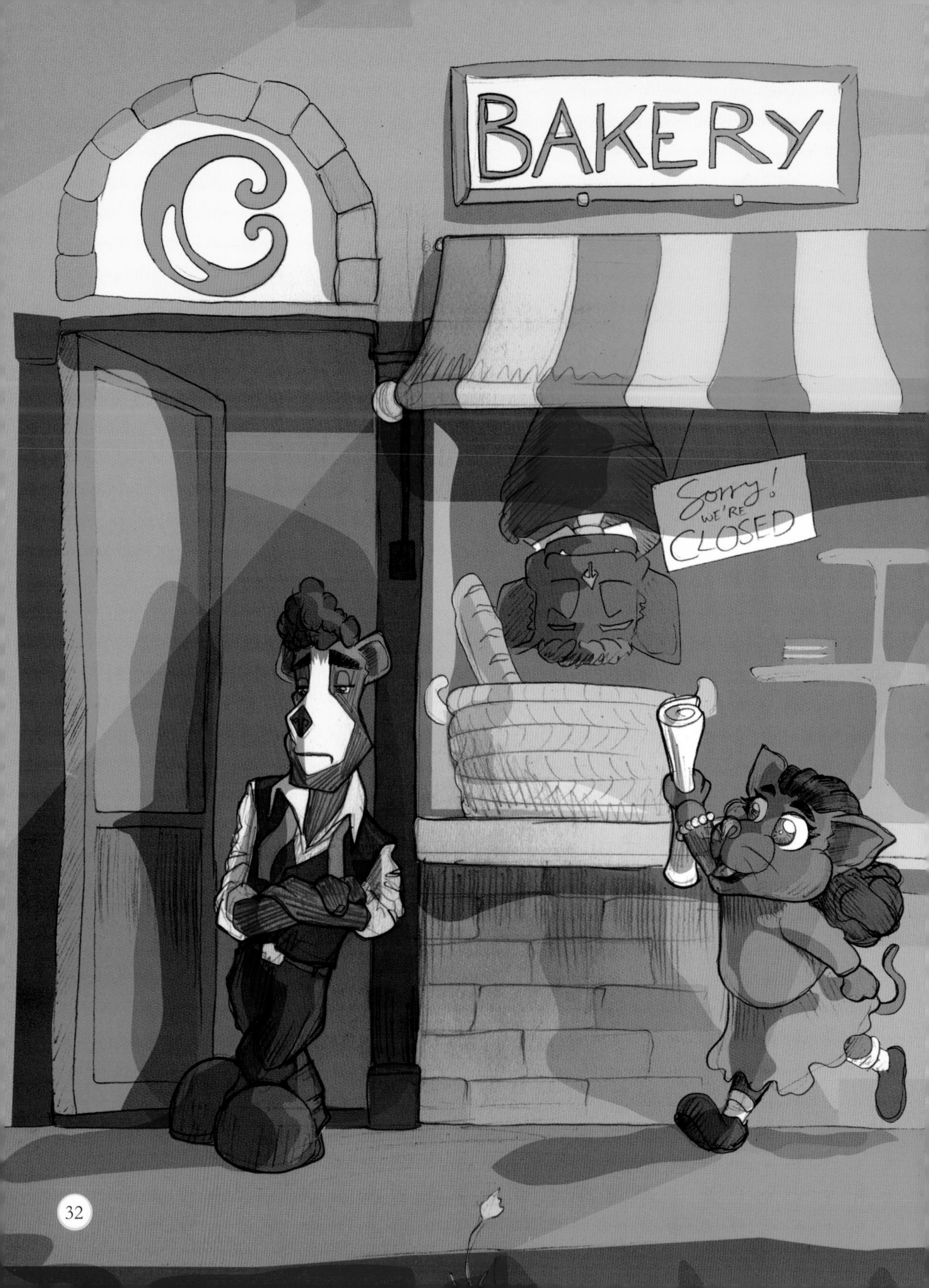
BAKERY
Sorry! WE'RE CLOSED

'Hear ye, hear ye! Let's cook, one and all.
Calling chefs of all shapes, big and small!
Now don't you flake off;
Prepare for the Cake-Off!
The champion will get a great windfall.'

Connie read breathlessly from the poster.
Sonny grabbed at it to see it up-closer.
'Don wins it every year,
But he's in bed, I fear,'
Said Tom. 'We can't win this time, no sir.'

Here is when Sonny decided to take charge,
Although Don's apron was far too large.
He grinned with some guilt
About the sugar he'd spilt.
And into the kitchen did Mama Cannoli barge.

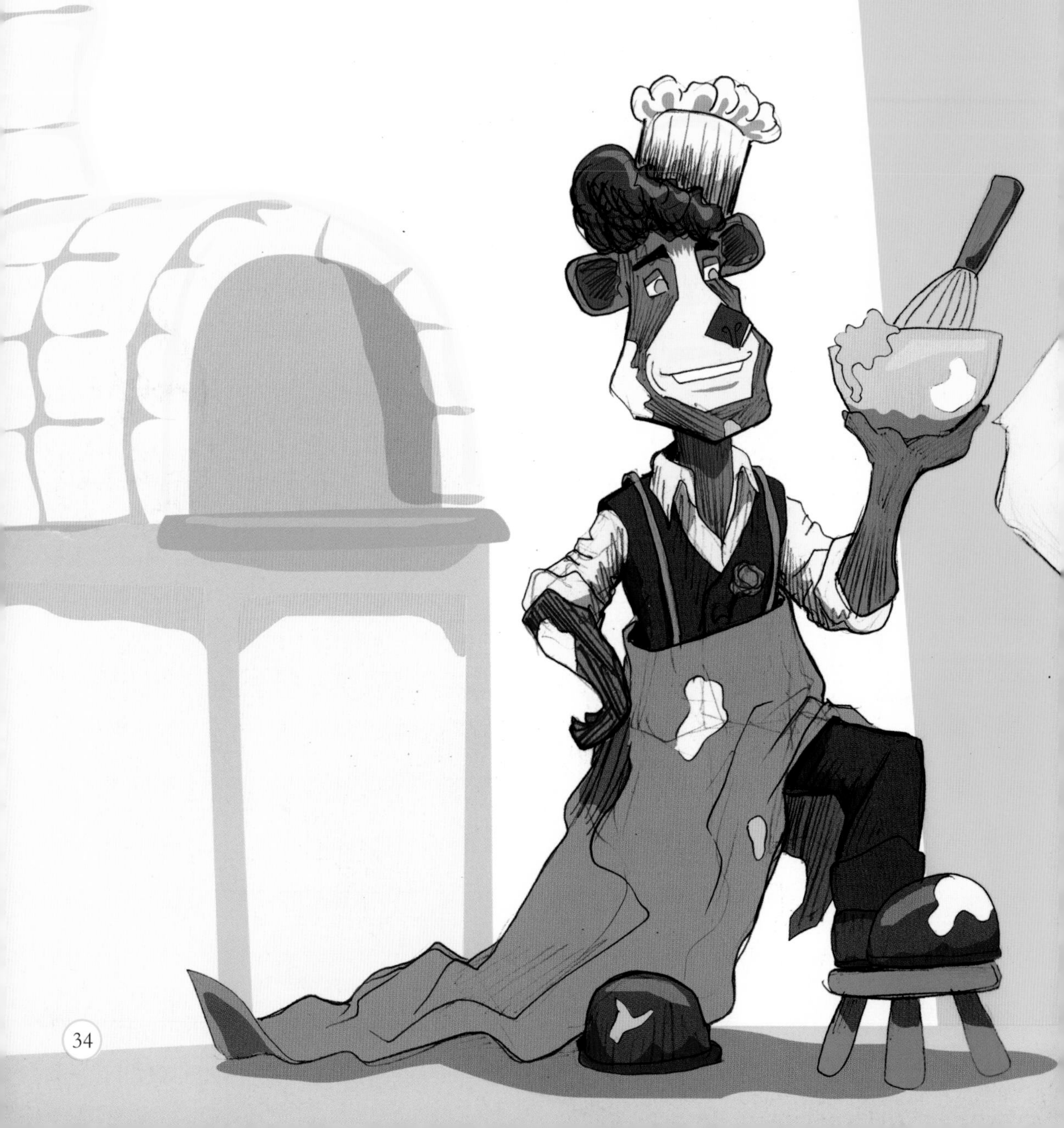

Mama loved feeding folks, just like Don did,
And she knew her help was very wanted.
Alas, she was better at pasta
Than making dessert faster,
So now she made sure her kids were well fed.

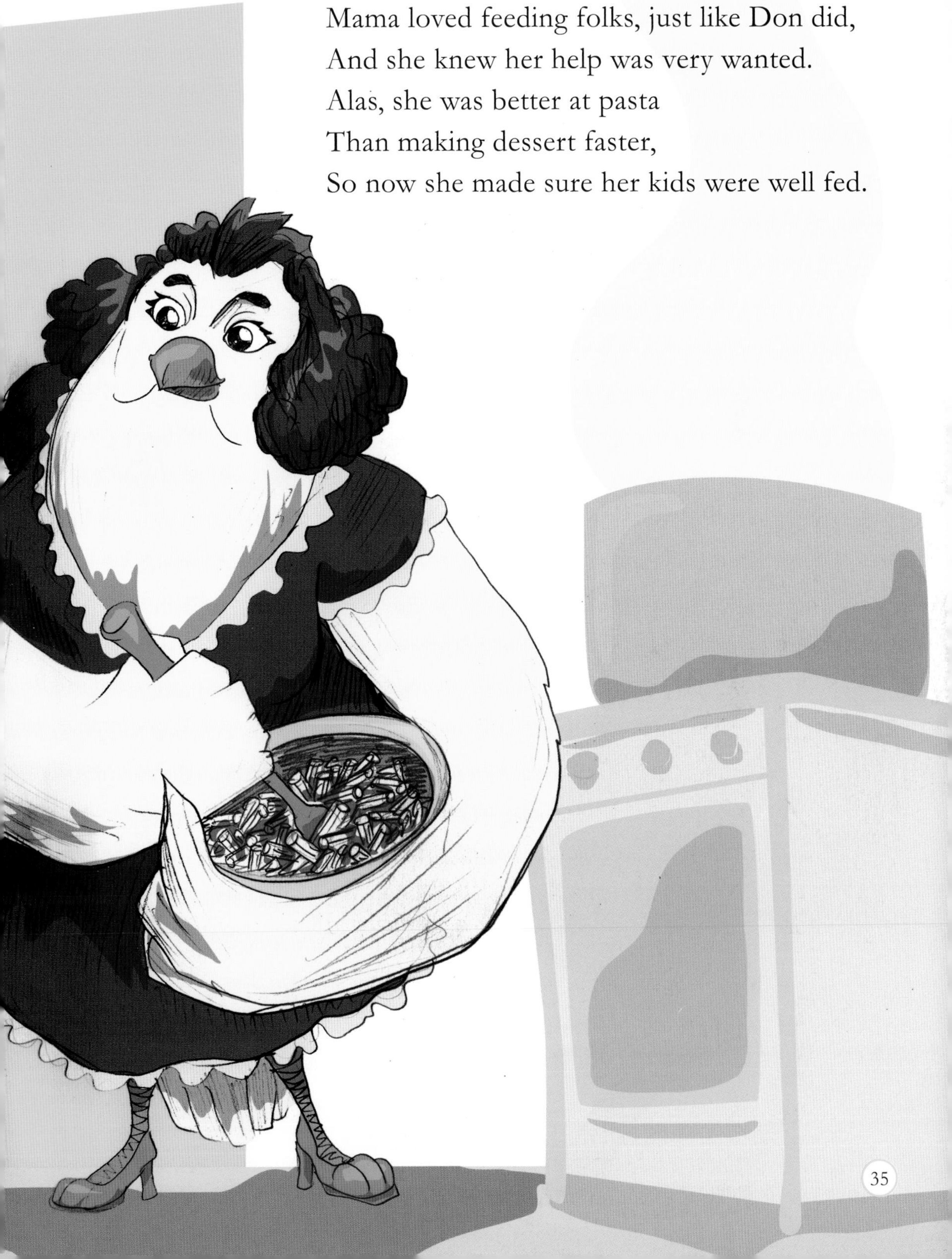

‘Someday you might have to cook for twenty guys,
So here’s what I suggest that, Michael, you try:
Fry some tomatoes, fry some garlic.
Careful, make sure they don’t stick.
Add sausages, meatballs and a bit of sugar, say I.’

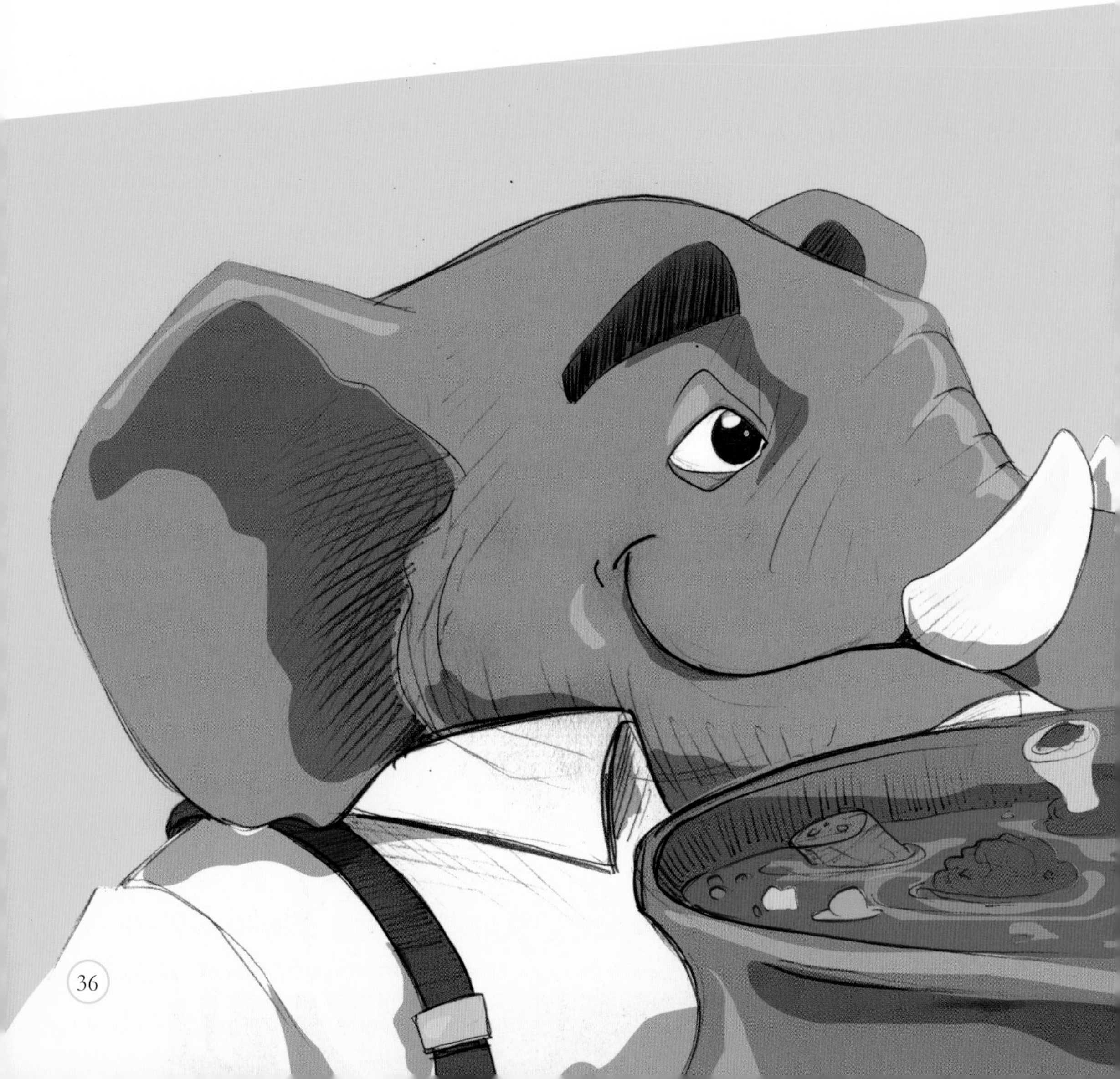

Clemenza gave Michael the lesson with a wink,
But young Mike was having a different think.
Getting an idea from meatballs,
He decided to stand tall,
And said he would face the Turk with the stink.

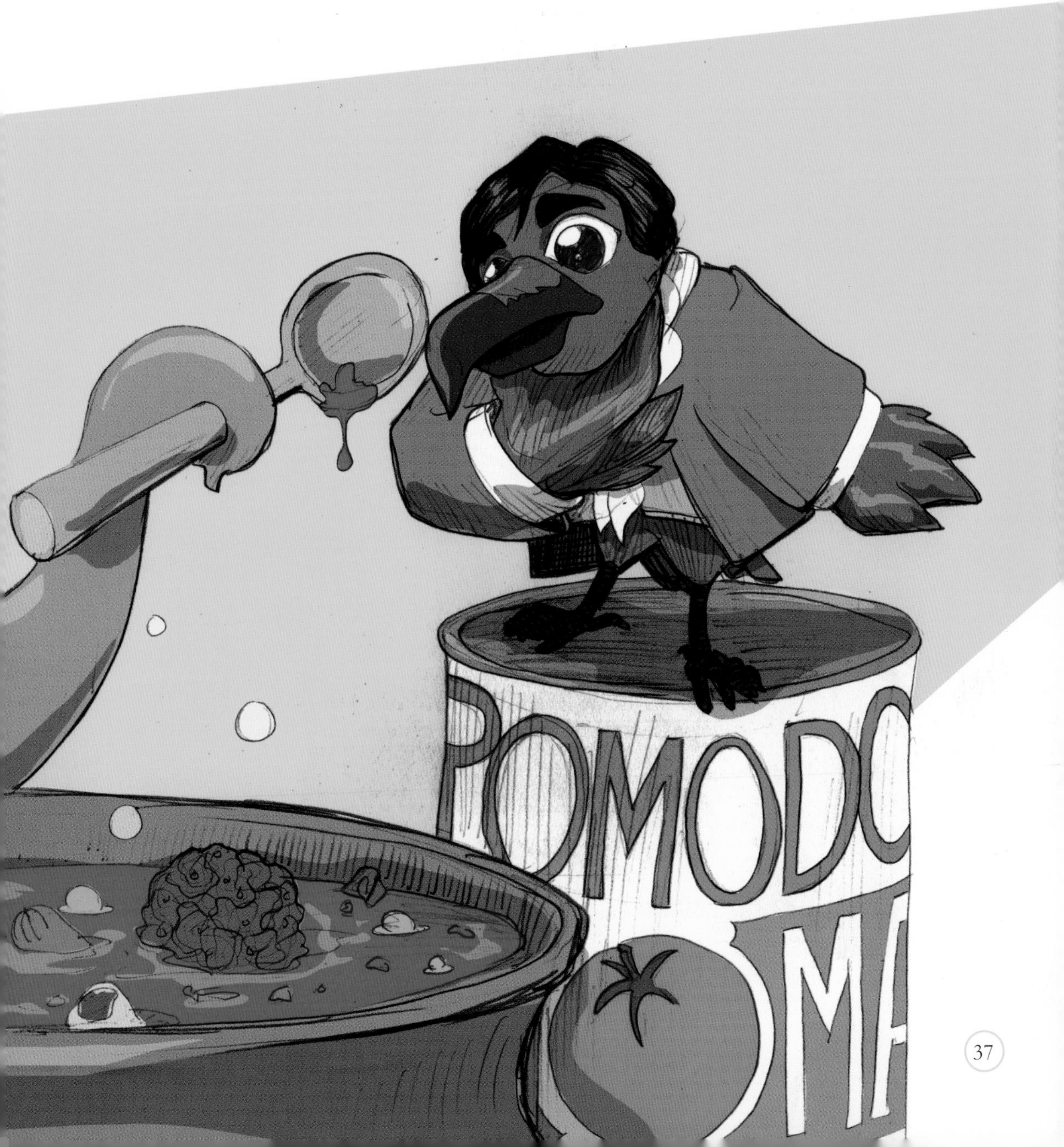
POMODO
MA

Sonny heard Michael and laughed and laughed.
He ba-da-bing'd his kid brother's idea so daft!
'It's business, not personal.
I know Papa's been ill,
But we have to handle this with some craft.'

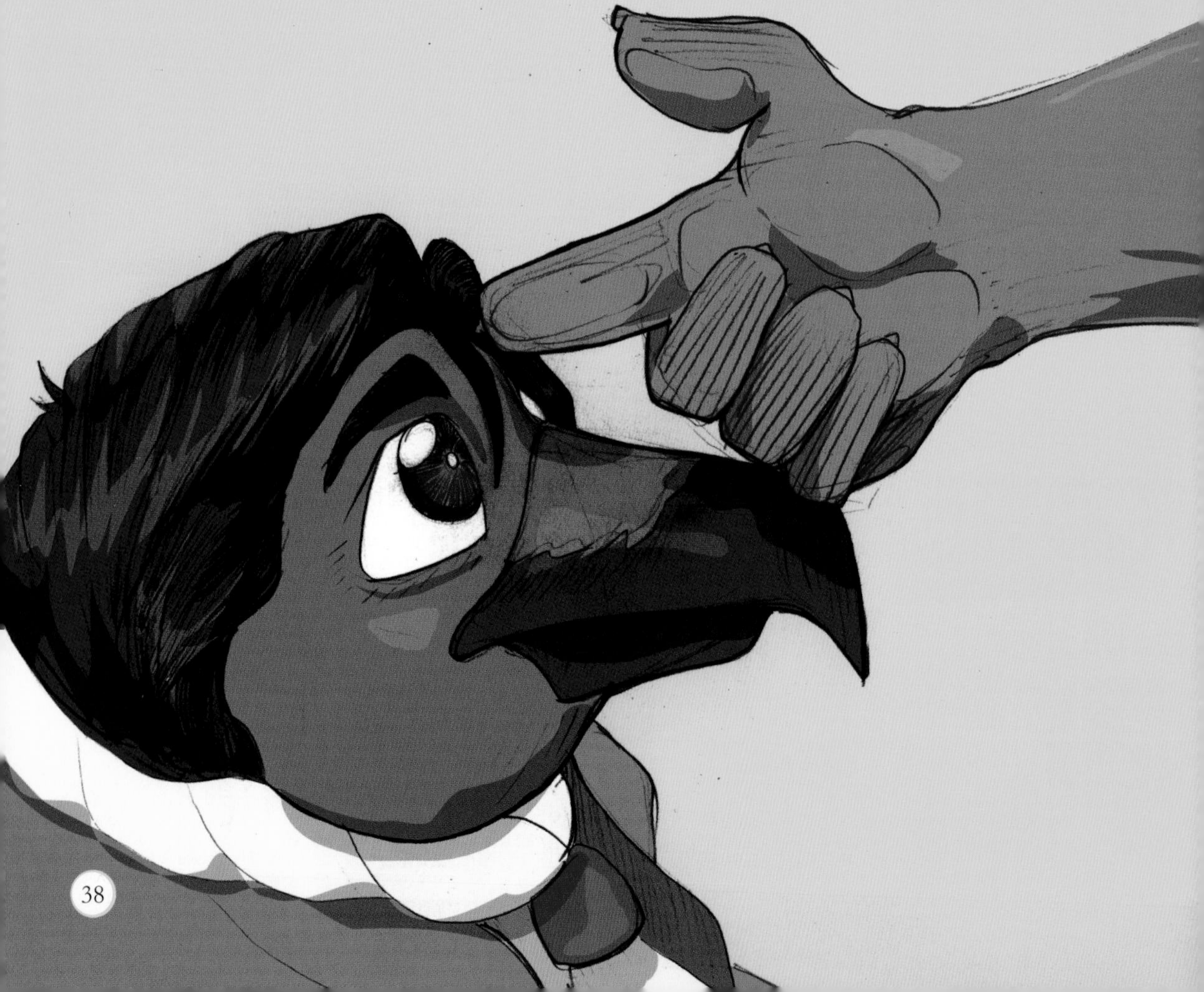

'Hang on, Sonny, this might actually be hot.
We know the Boy Scout can handle a slingshot.'
Tom took Michael's side,
Big Clemenza did abide.
They said they'd hide his weapon behind the pot.

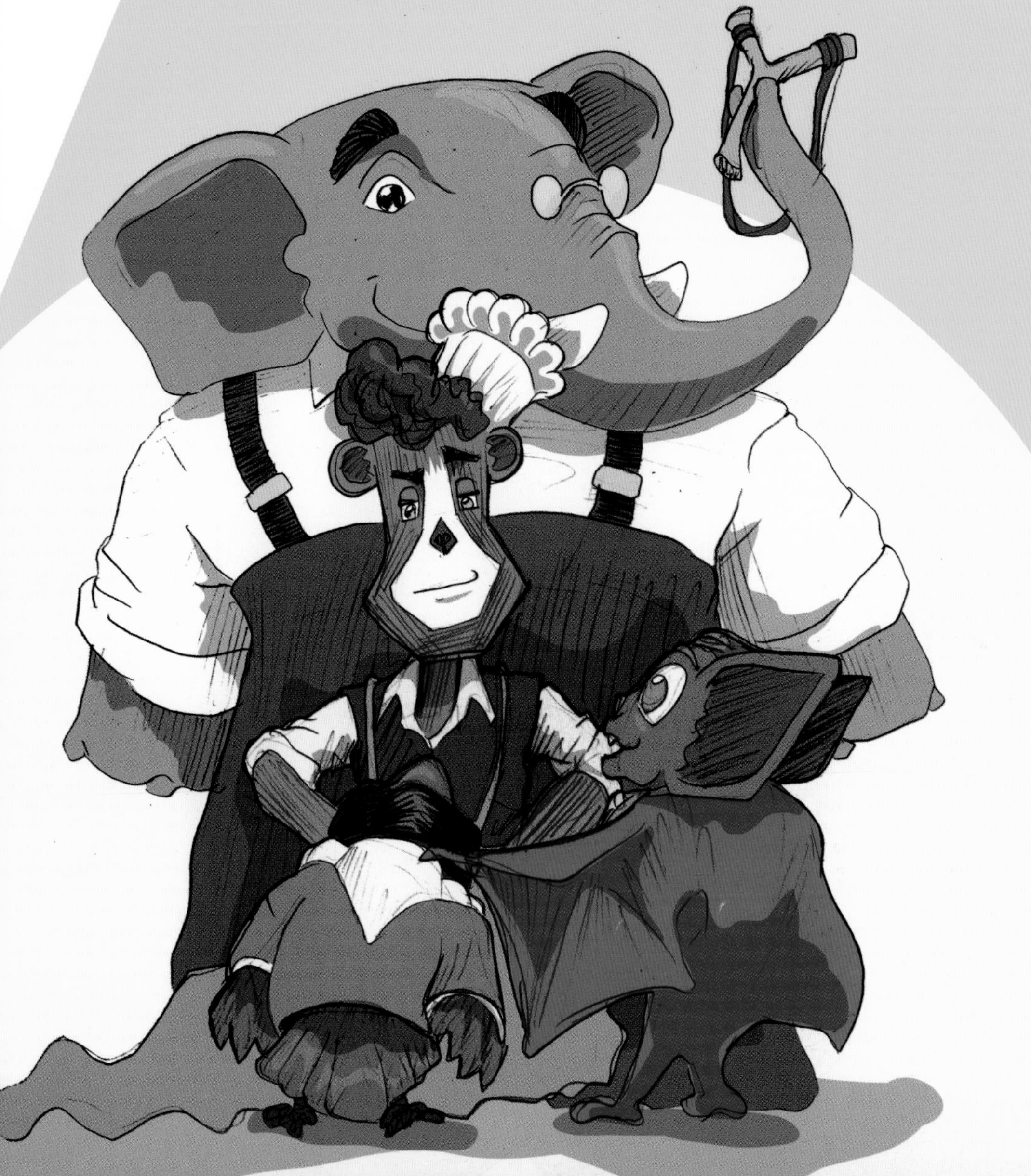

’Tis then, on that fateful dinner night,
When Michael sits to the Turk’s right,
The villain noisily slurps
Spaghetti and then burps.
And young Michael readies for a fight.

Mike excuses himself for a while because
To fetch his slingshot he needs a pause.
He loads a big meatball,
And before Turk can brawl,
Shoots the hard-candy man in the schnoz!

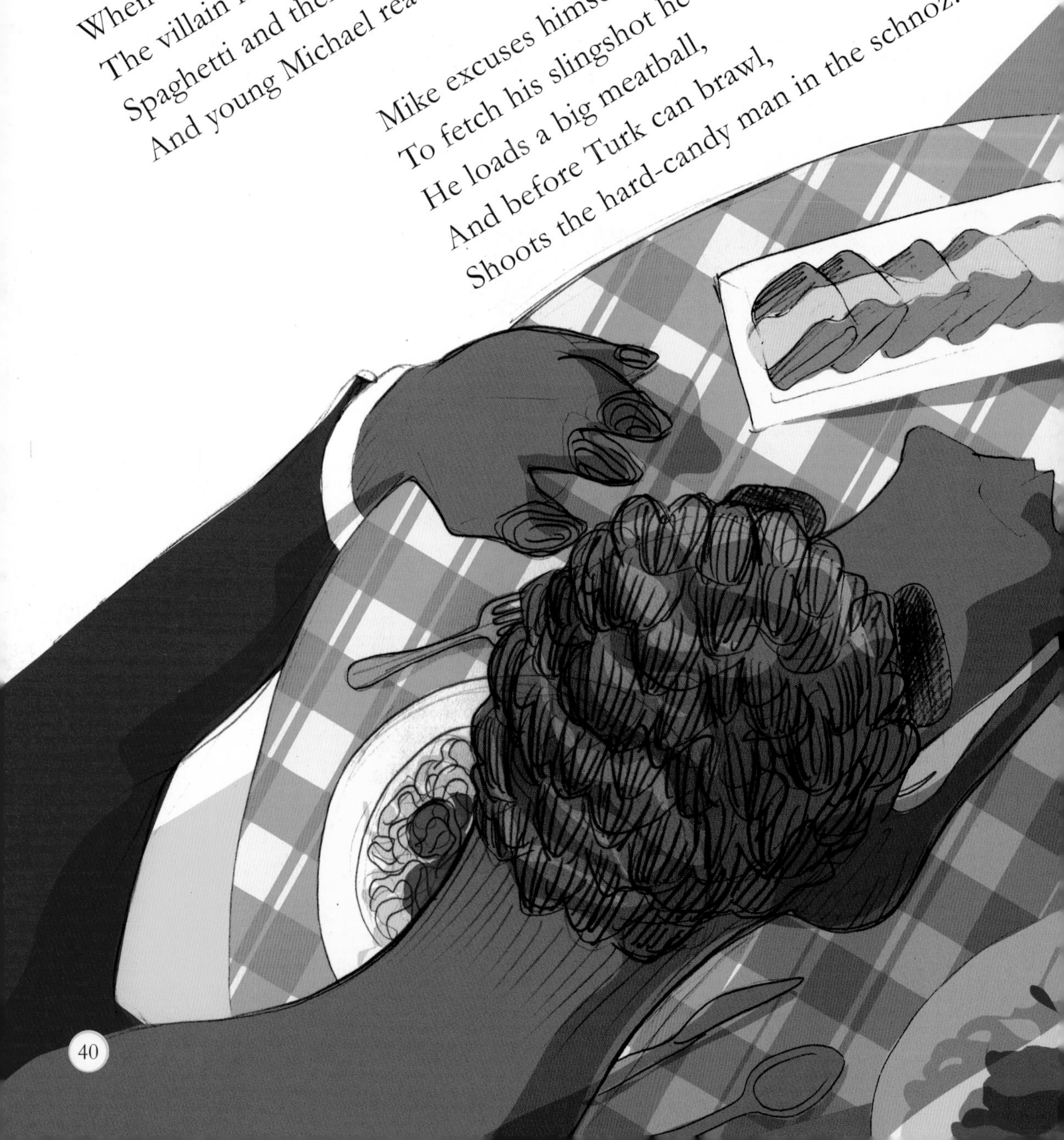

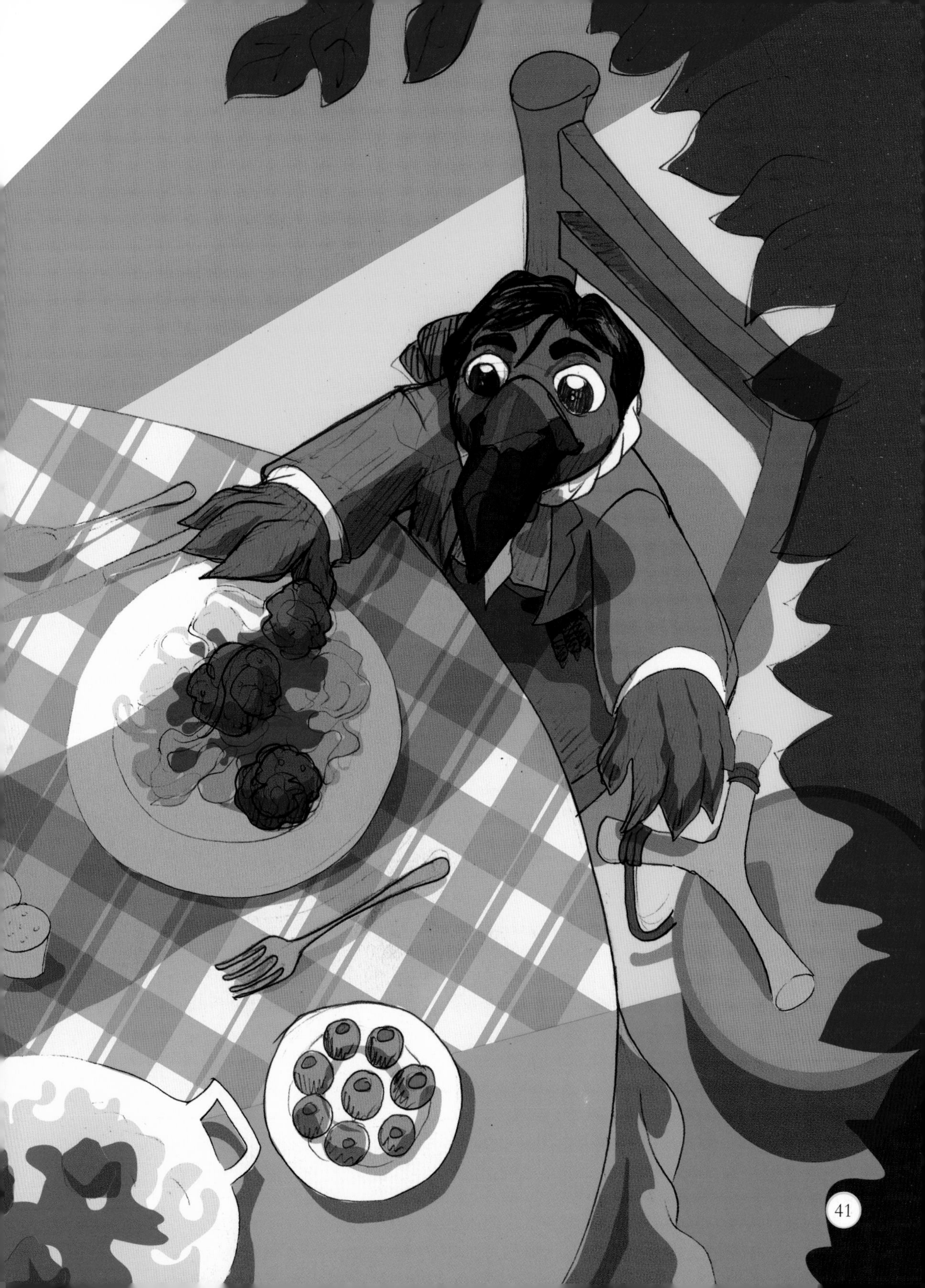

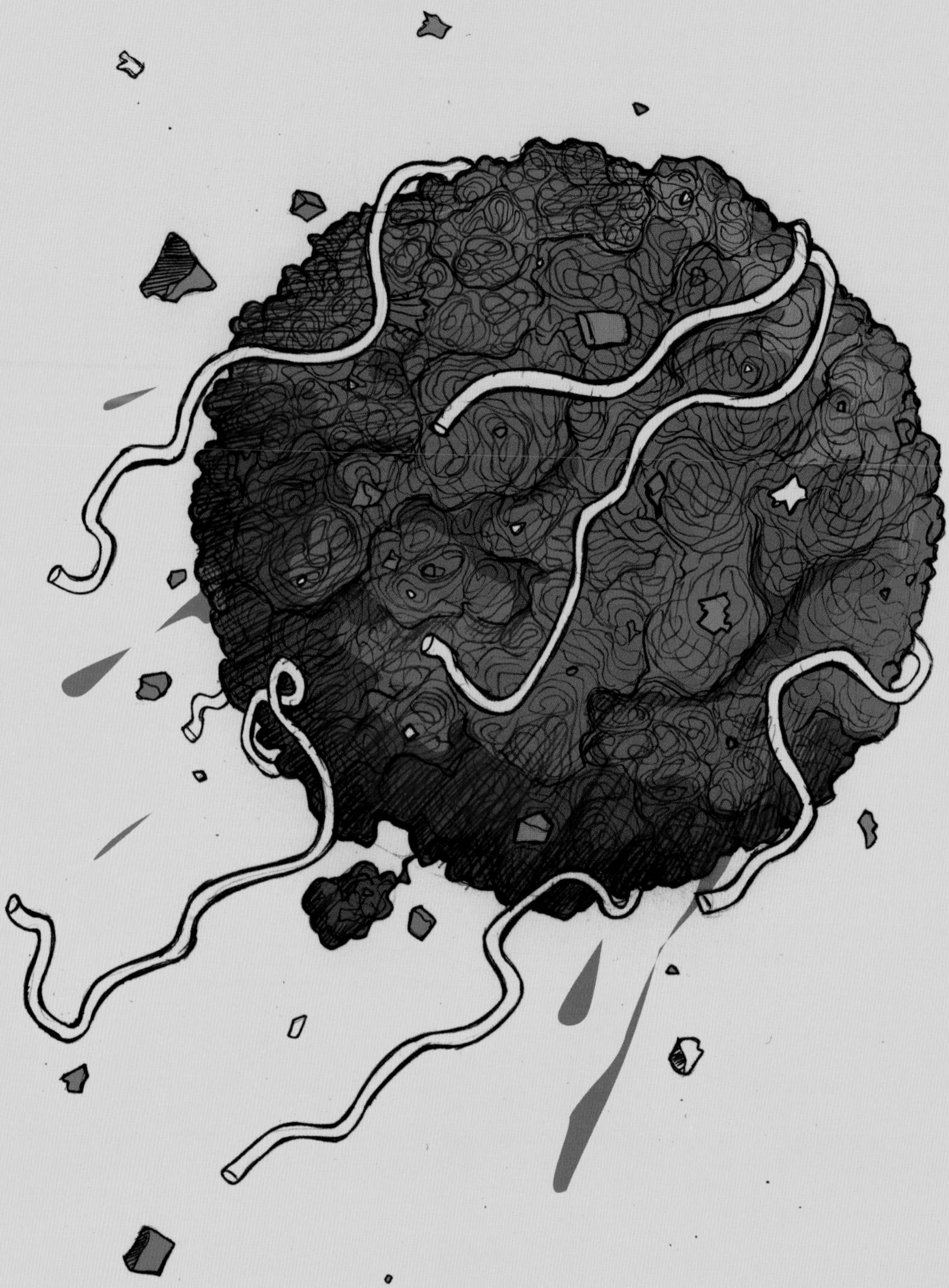

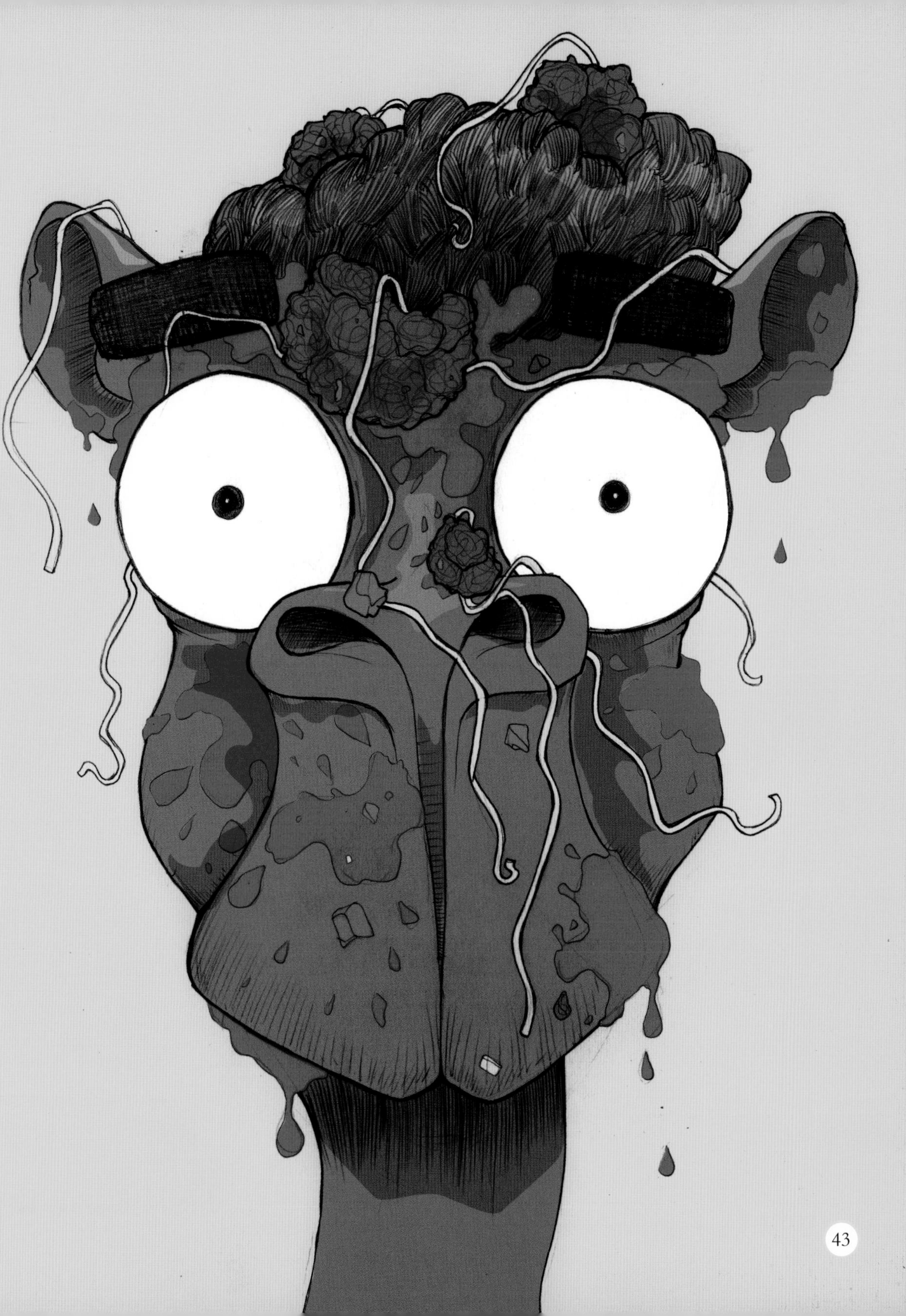

It was unusual to see the Don sitting up in bed.
He was (mostly) spotted in the kitchen instead.
But right then he was grim.
Standing in front of him
Was a trembling Michael,
fearing for his head.

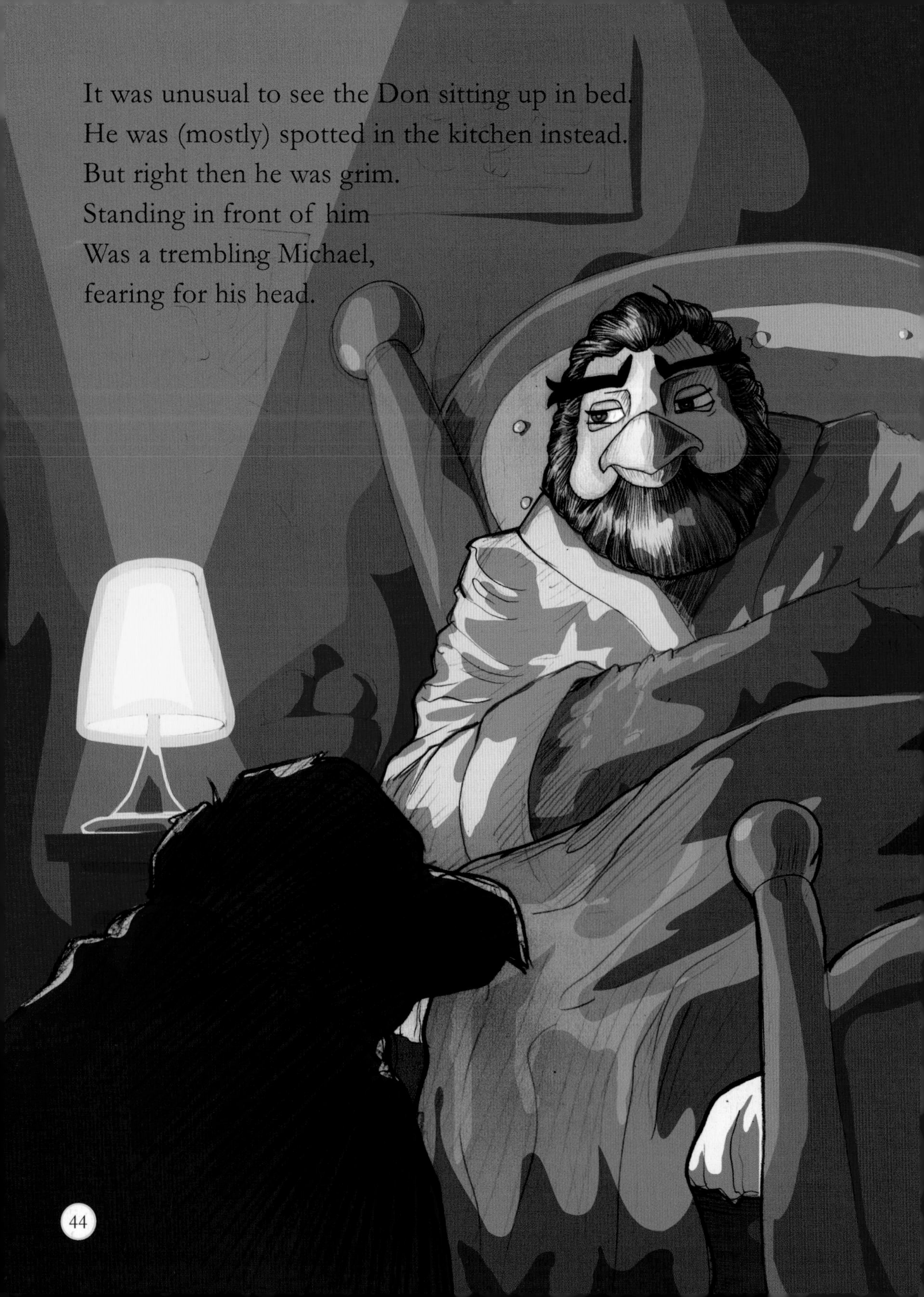

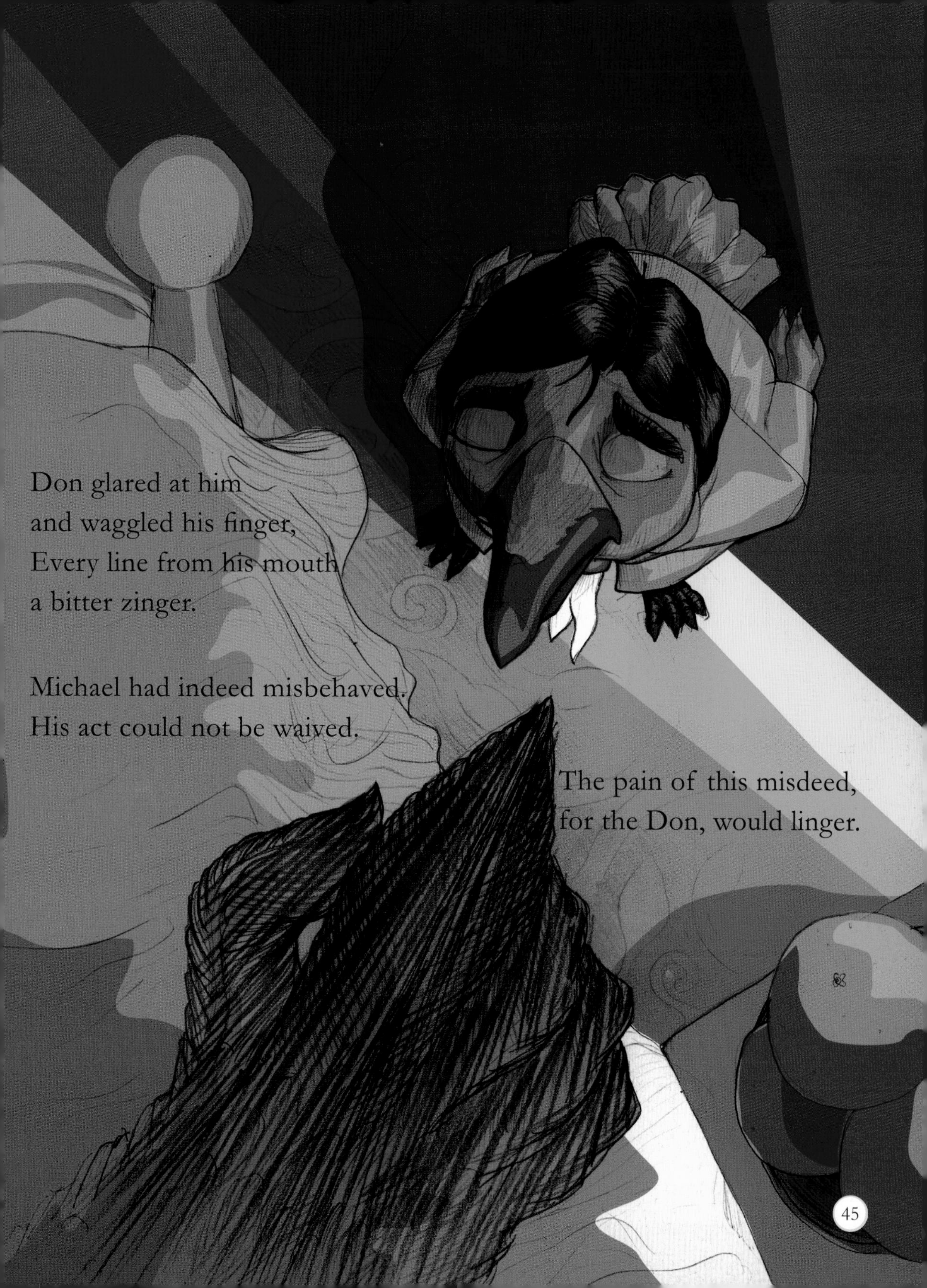

Don glared at him
and waggled his finger,
Every line from his mouth
a bitter zinger.

Michael had indeed misbehaved.
His act could not be waived.

The pain of this misdeed,
for the Don, would linger.

'Never go against the principles of the family,
Even if avenging the principals of the family.'
Thus did the Don admonish
And decided he must banish
Michael to his room
without cake or telly.

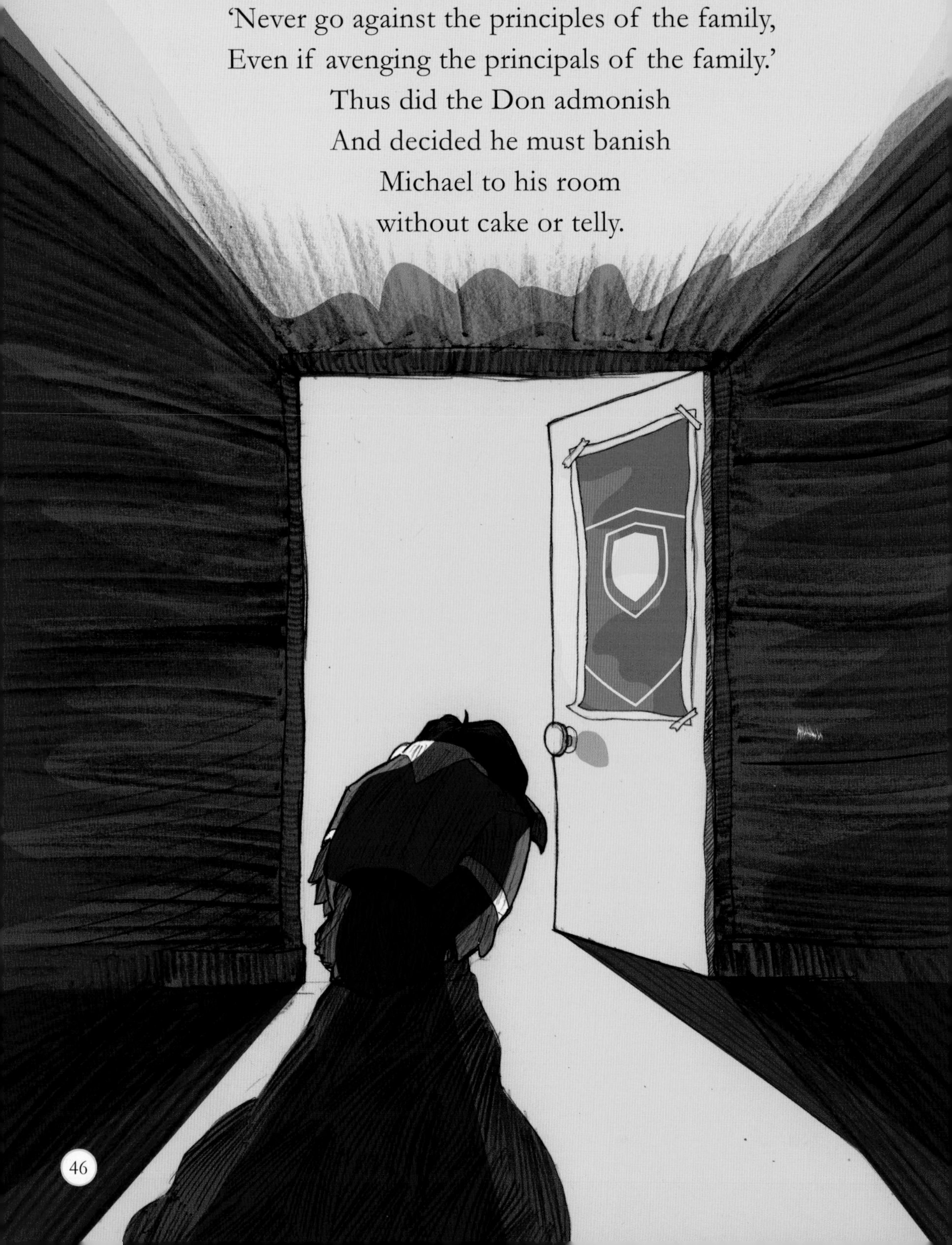

Meanwhile, Sonny clumsily continued to lead,
Messing up recipes he wouldn't (fully) read.

He got angrier as he failed,
Against his friends he flailed,

Yelling at Tessio
and Connie
and Tom to succeed.

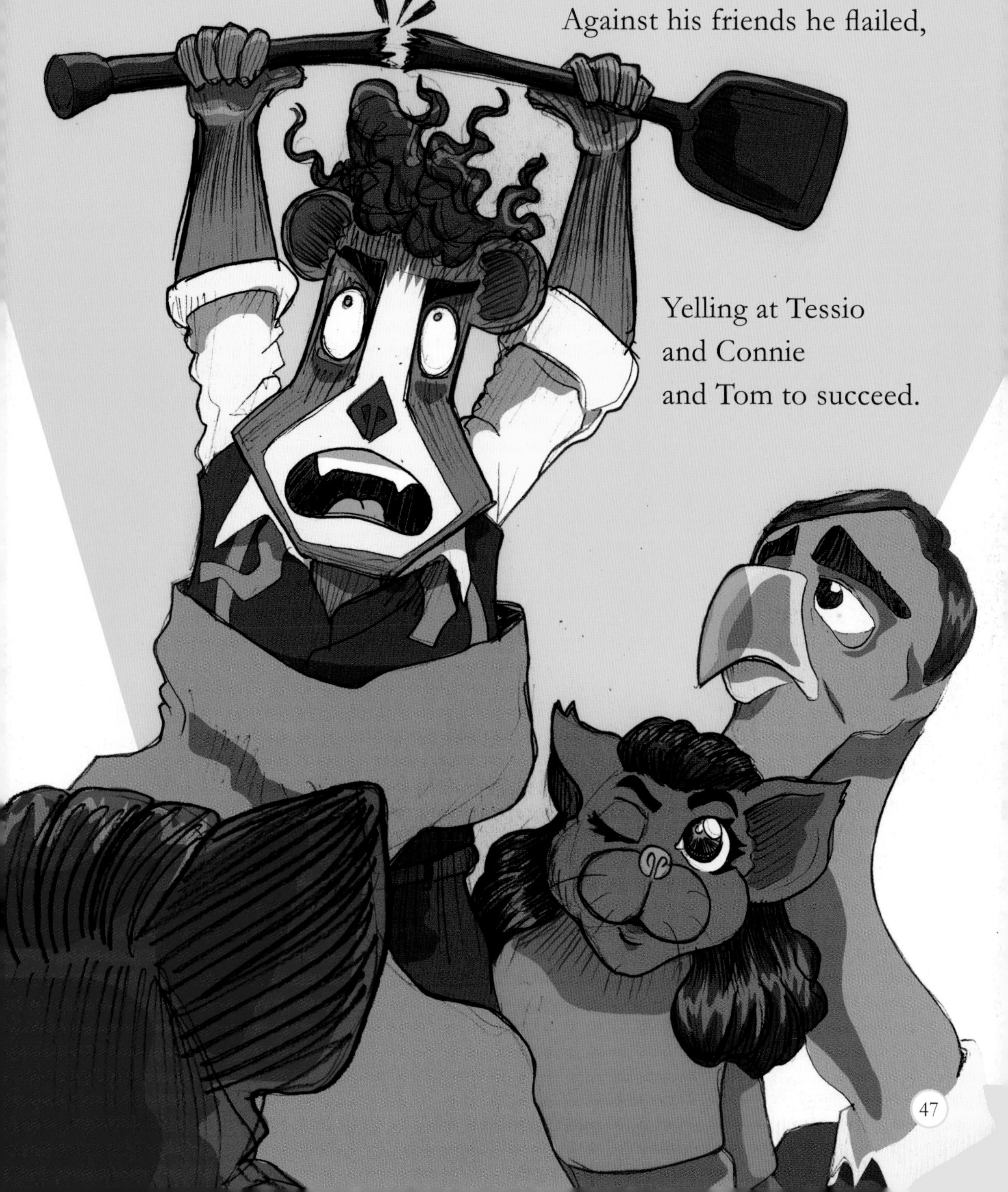

One day, with Sonny in a giant flour-flurry,
Tessio flew into the kitchen and said, 'Hurry!
Something's gone wrong.
Come, come on along;
There's no time and the others will worry!'

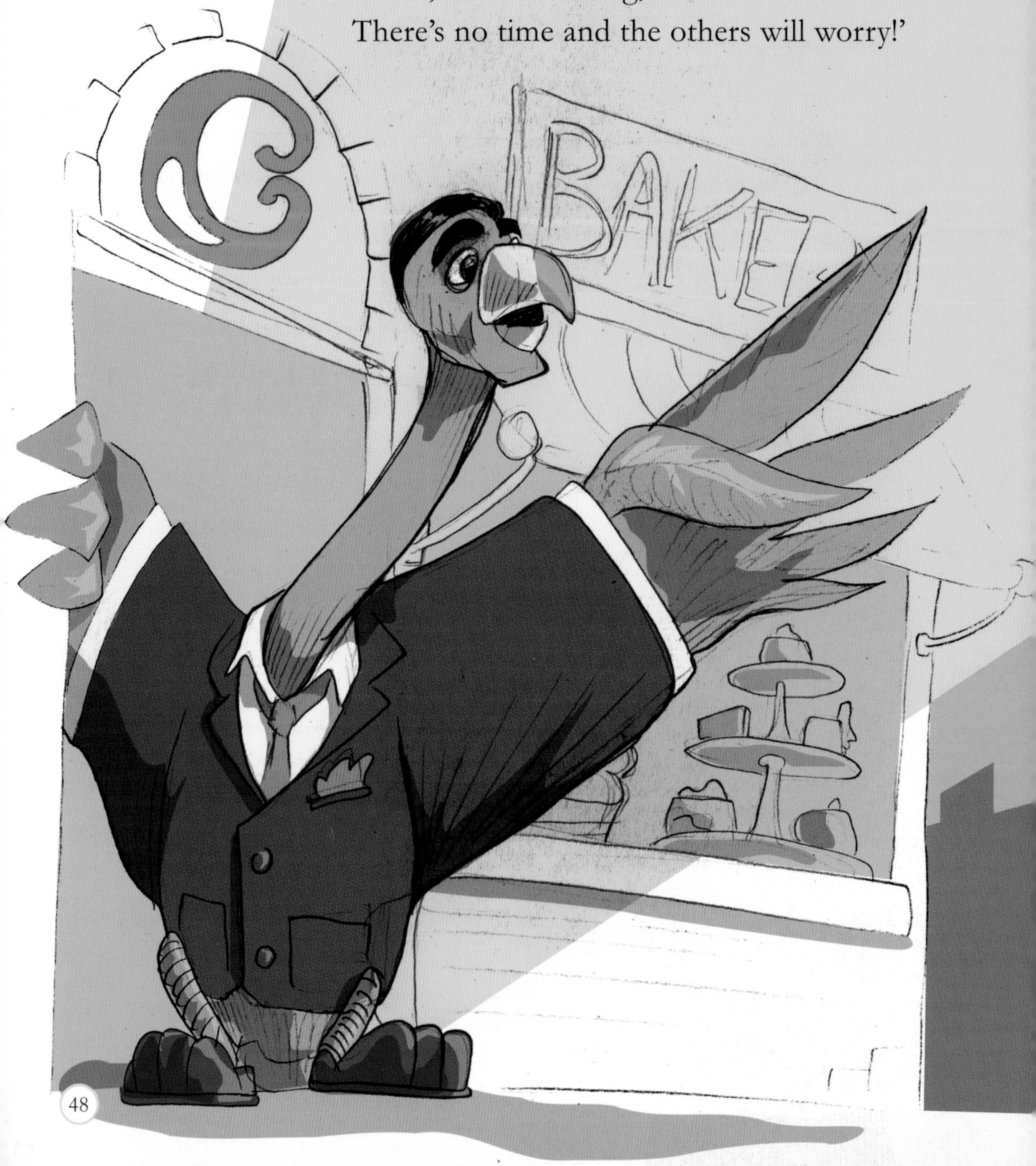

Sonny ran out, alone, without any defence.
Angry young 'uns stood in line, looking tense.

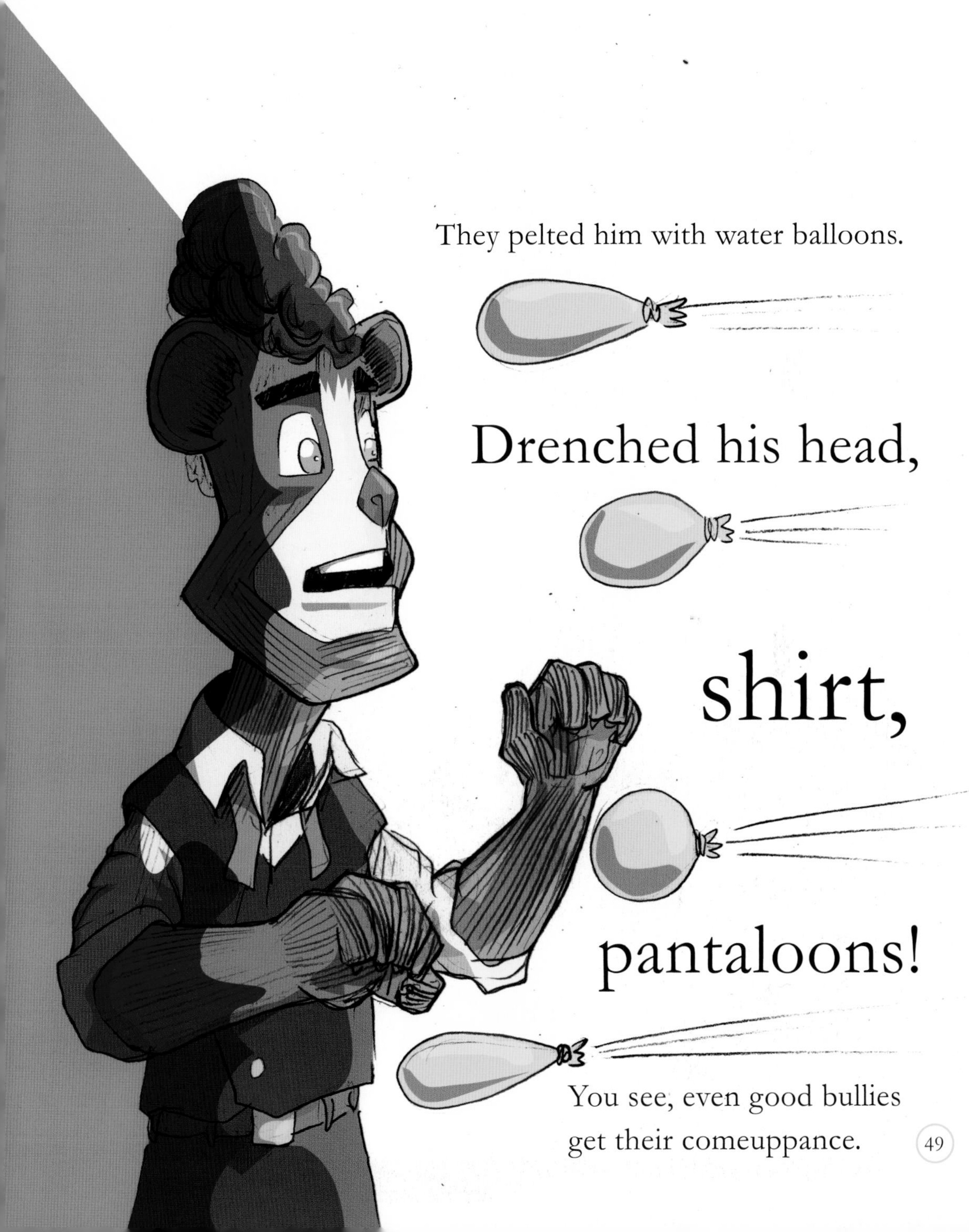

They pelted him with water balloons.

Drenched his head,

shirt,

pantaloons!

You see, even good bullies
get their comeuppance.

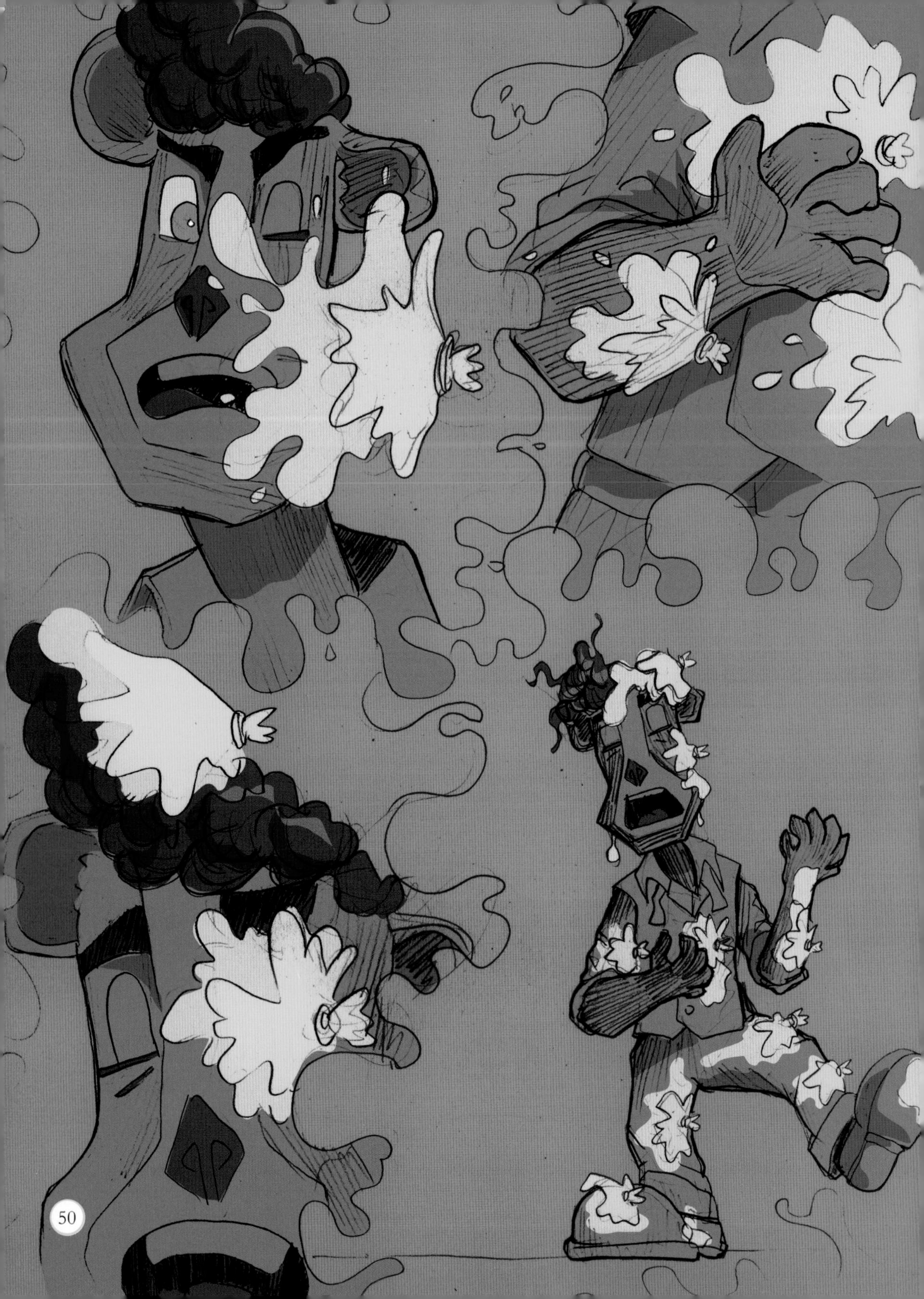

'Look how they soaked my boy,' the Don cried,
While big, tough Sonny sniffled by his side.
With them laid up in bed,
The contest was as good as dead,
Till the kids appealed to the Don's sense of pride.

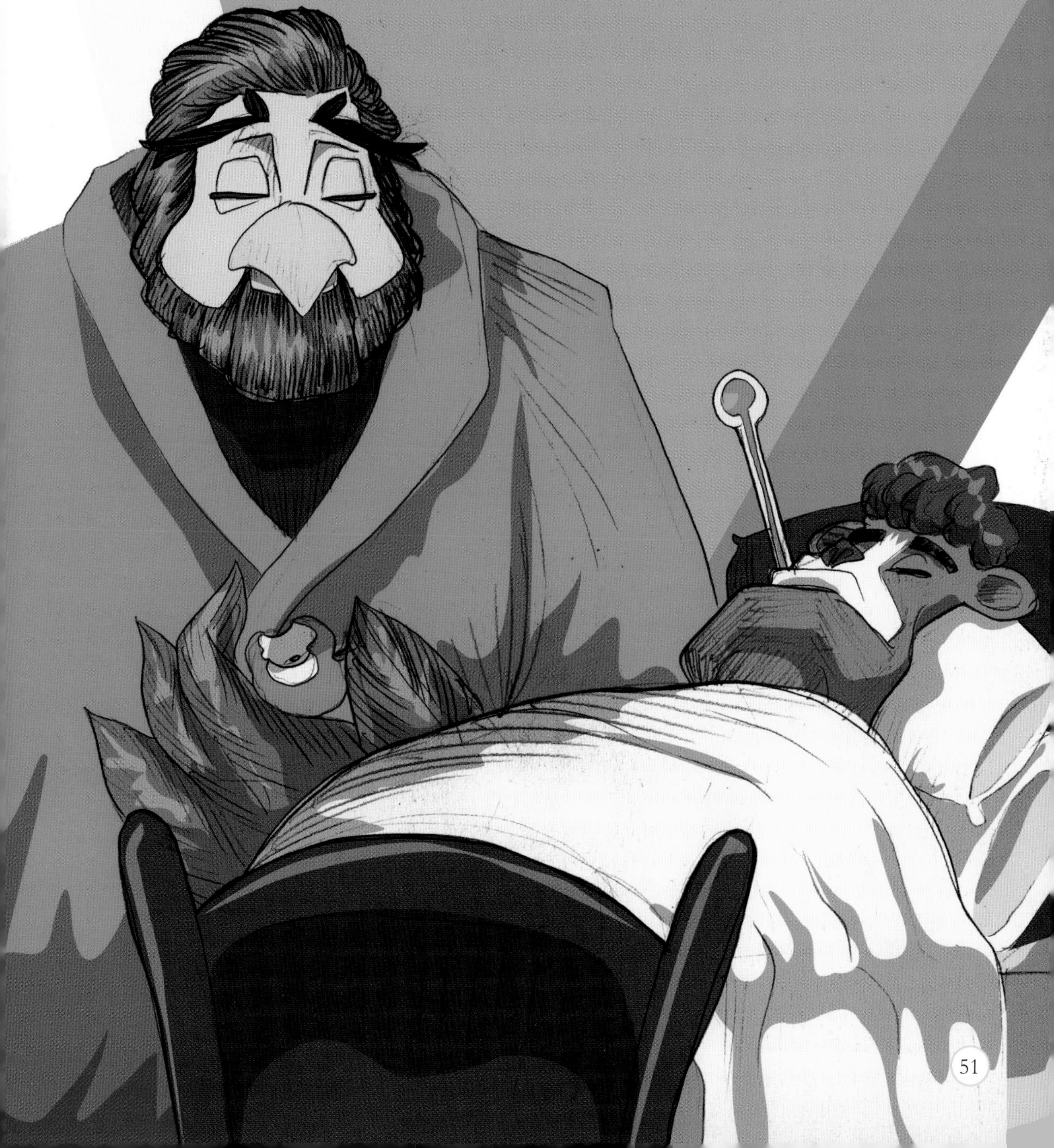

They swore and promised they'd make it happen;
They'd try and learn to get real good at bakin'!
The Don, impressed,
Puffed out his grand chest,
And told the Cake-Off team his kids would captain.

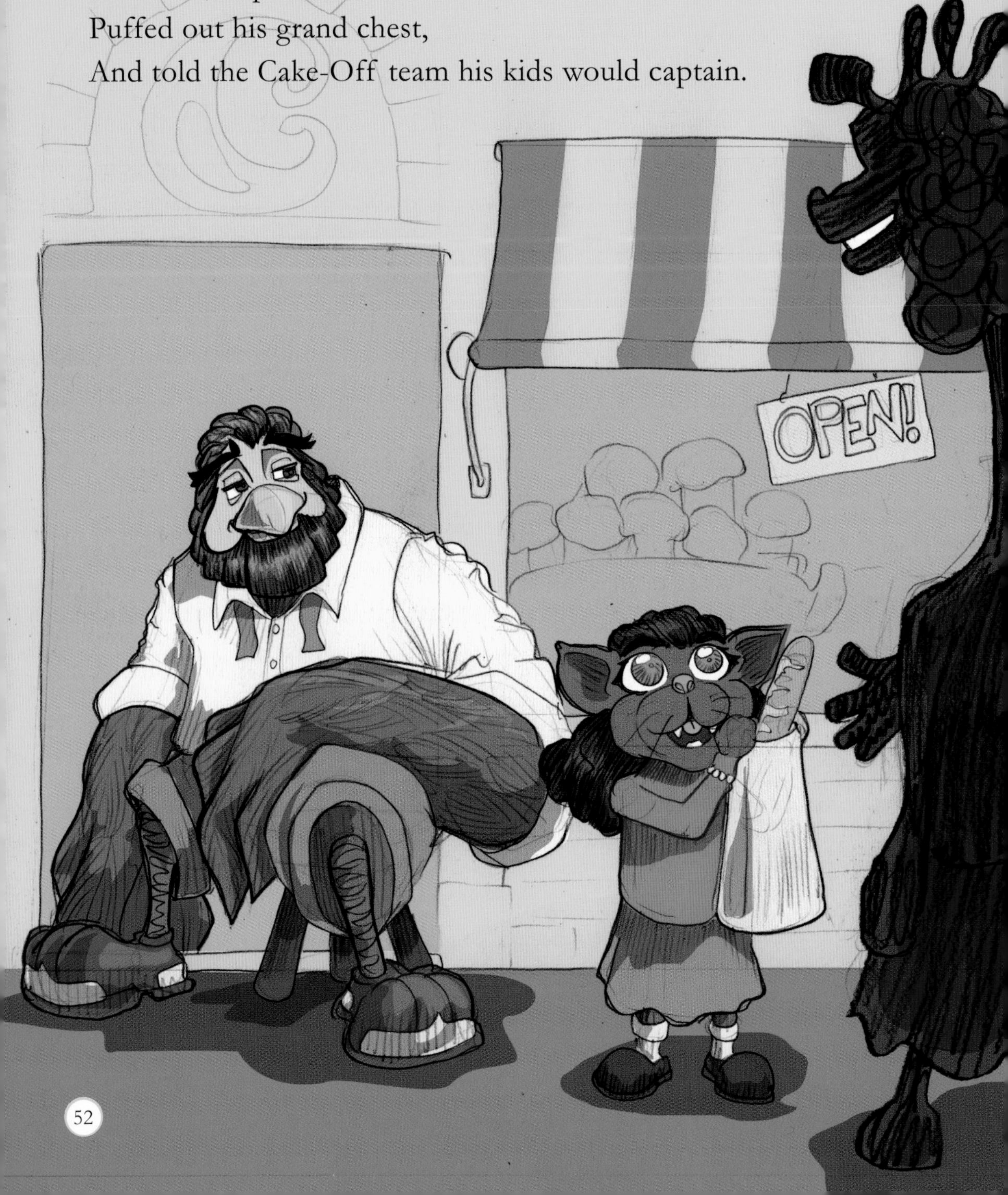
OPEN!

While the Cannolis were stuck in recovery mode,
Turk's candies had become popular along the road.
Hooked on the hard stuff,
Kids couldn't get enough.
Someone even saw Judge Francis lick a sugar toad!

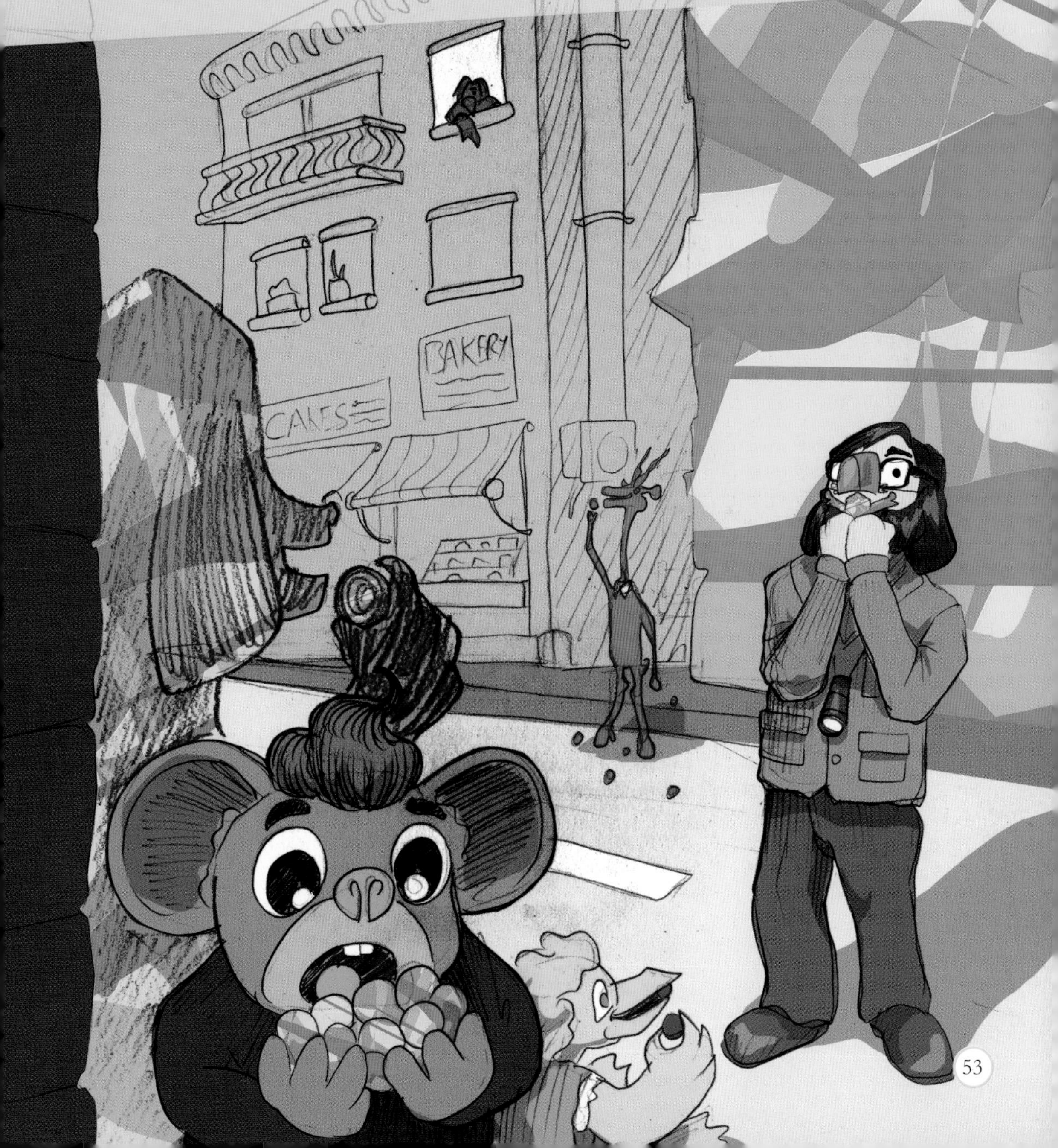
BAKERY
CAKES

The Don called a family meeting in order to assign a
Role for every person, since he liked plans to be finer.
He said, 'Enjoy baking for a while.
Serve the customers with a smile.

I'm going to get oranges
that come all the way from China.'

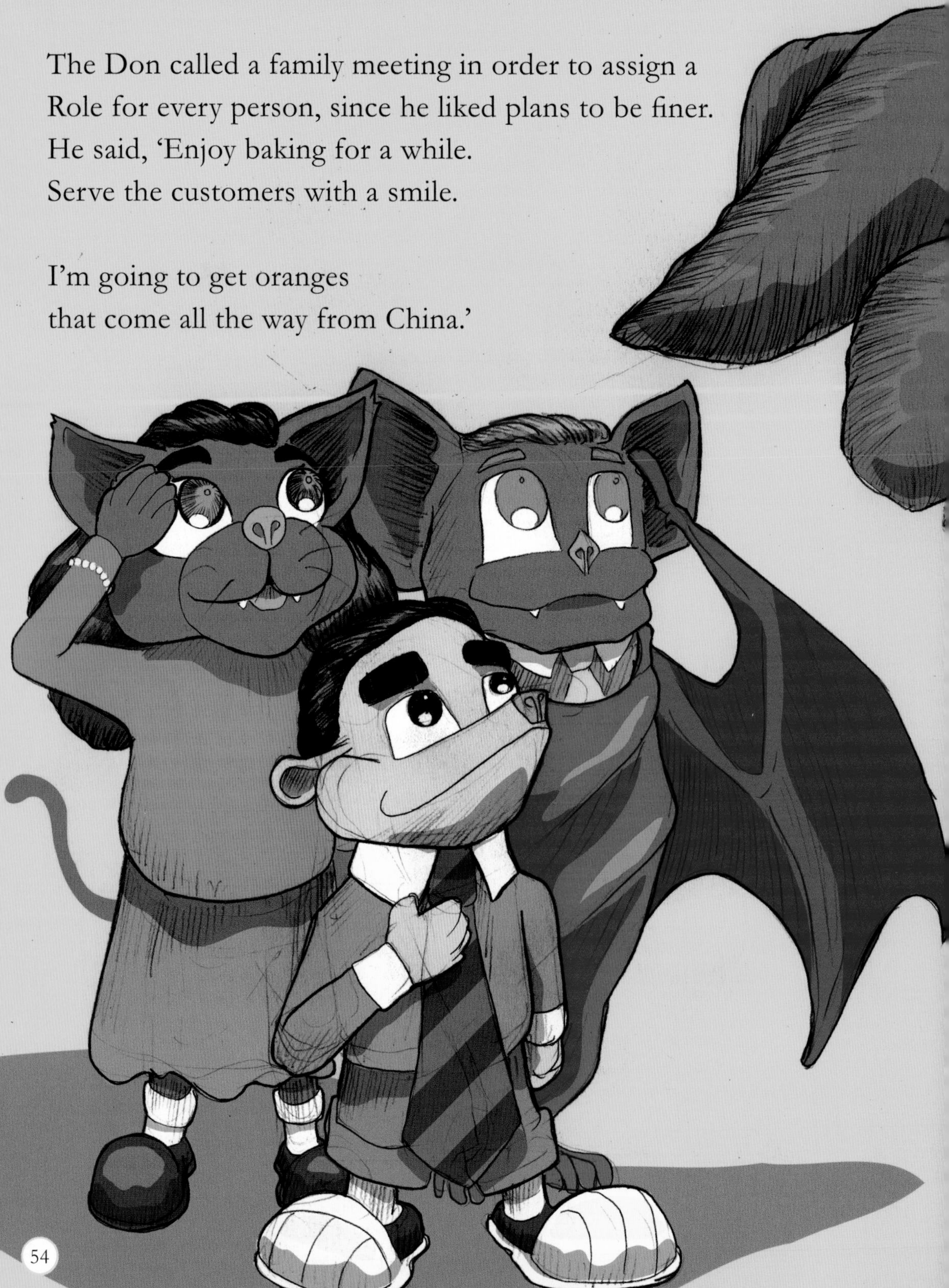

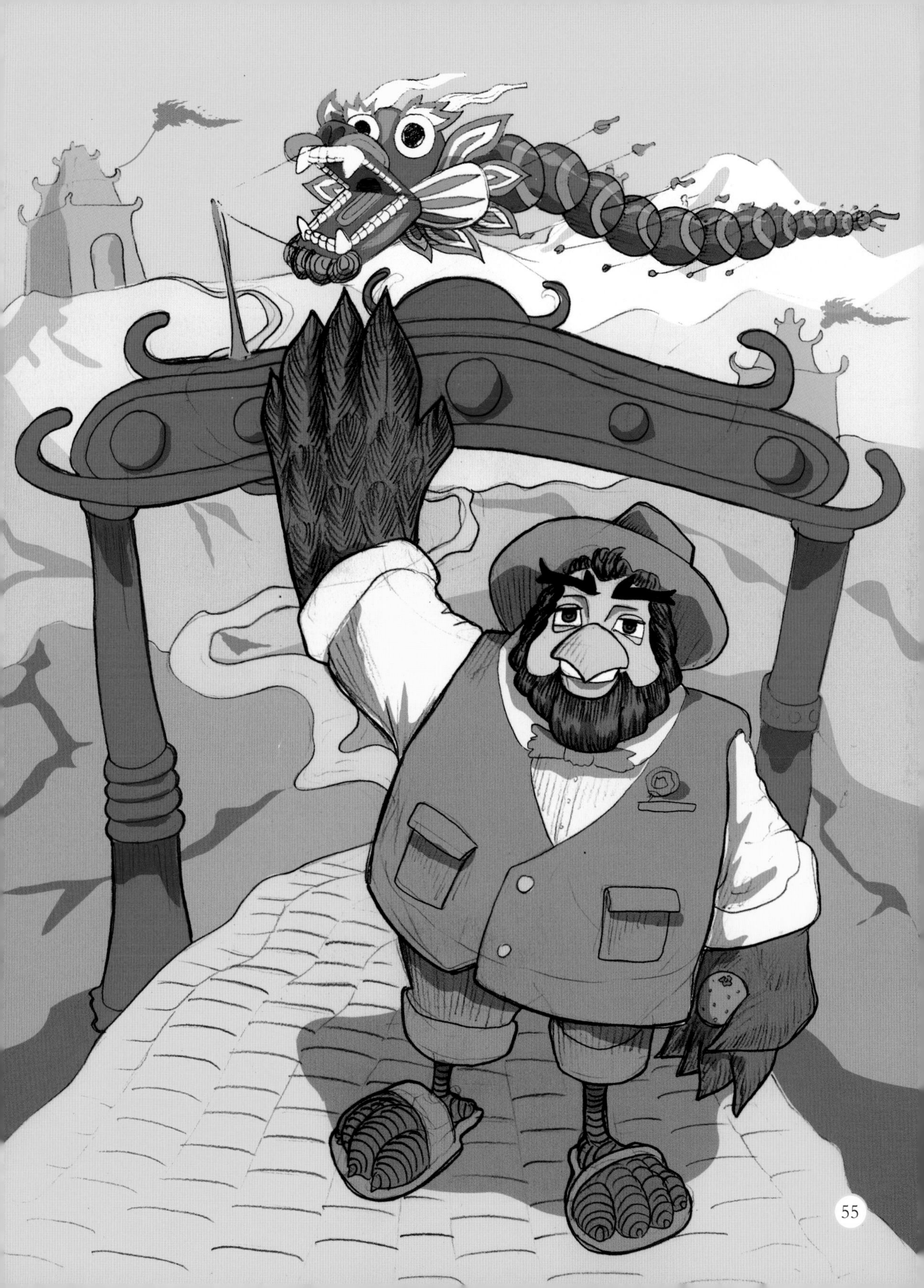

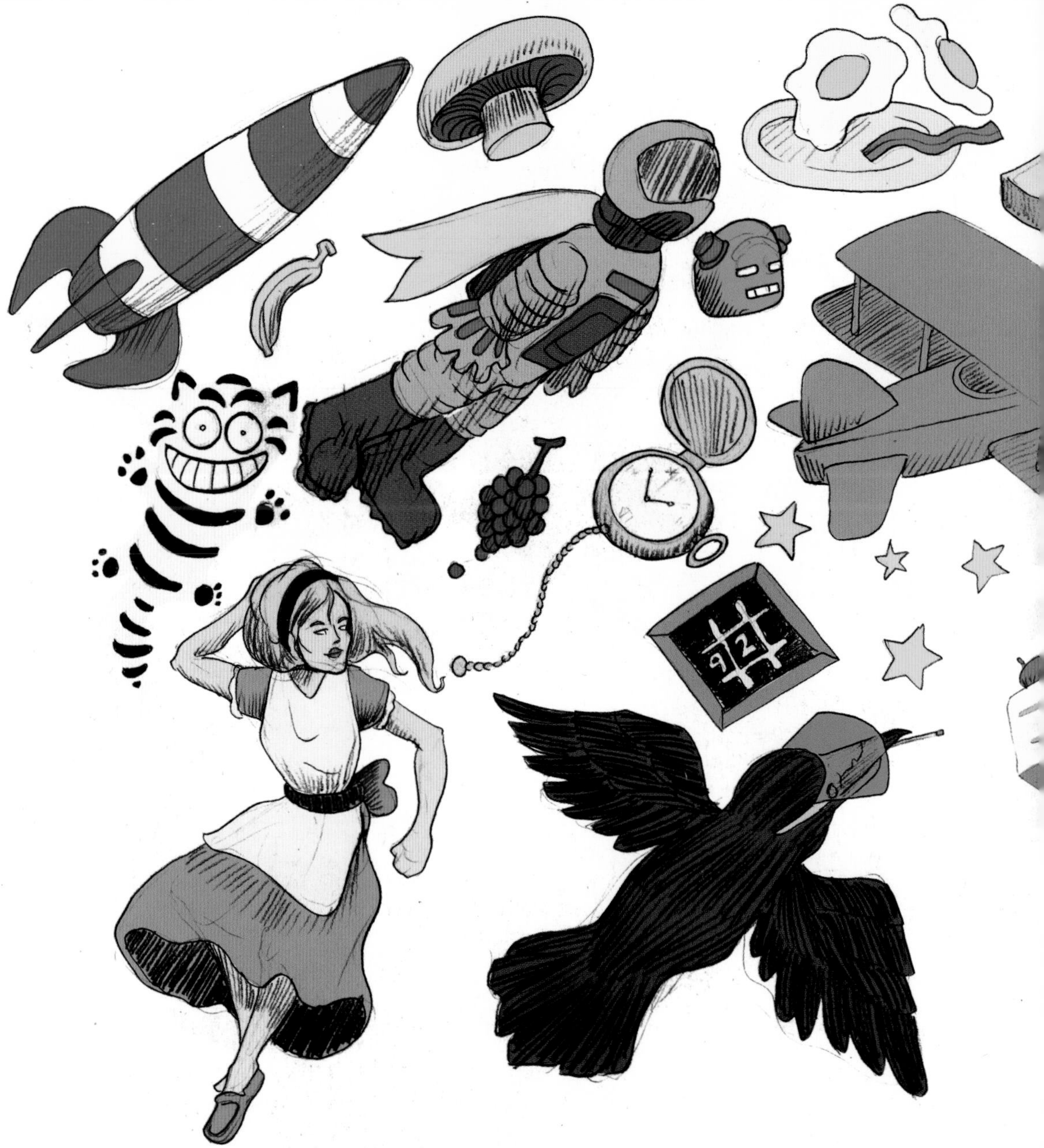

At first, Michael, in his room, was feeling trapped.
Then, to escape, he found himself in books, rapt.
Reading about a prince and a pilot,
And a girl chasing after a rabbit,
Till Kay sent him a cookbook, gift-wrapped.

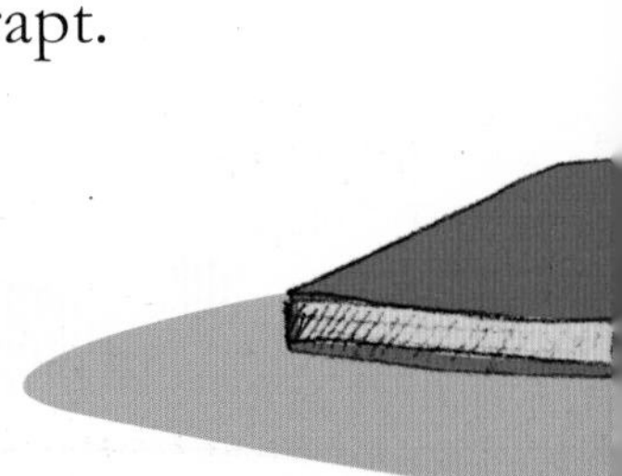

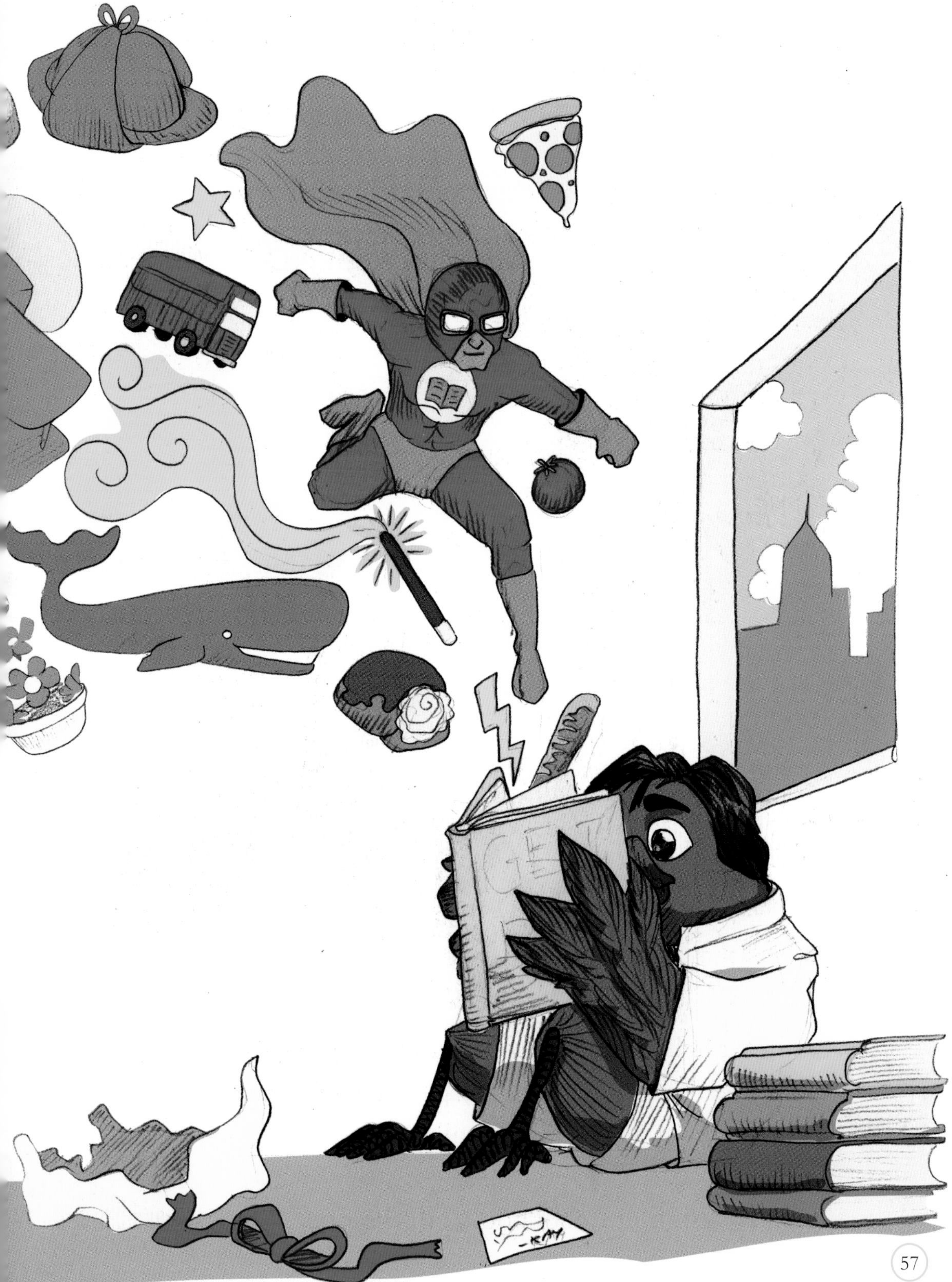

Michael came back down and the kids did gather
Under the parental mattress to plan the matter
Of the contest and the dish.
(And why Luca reeked of fish,
Because families must make time for idle chatter.)

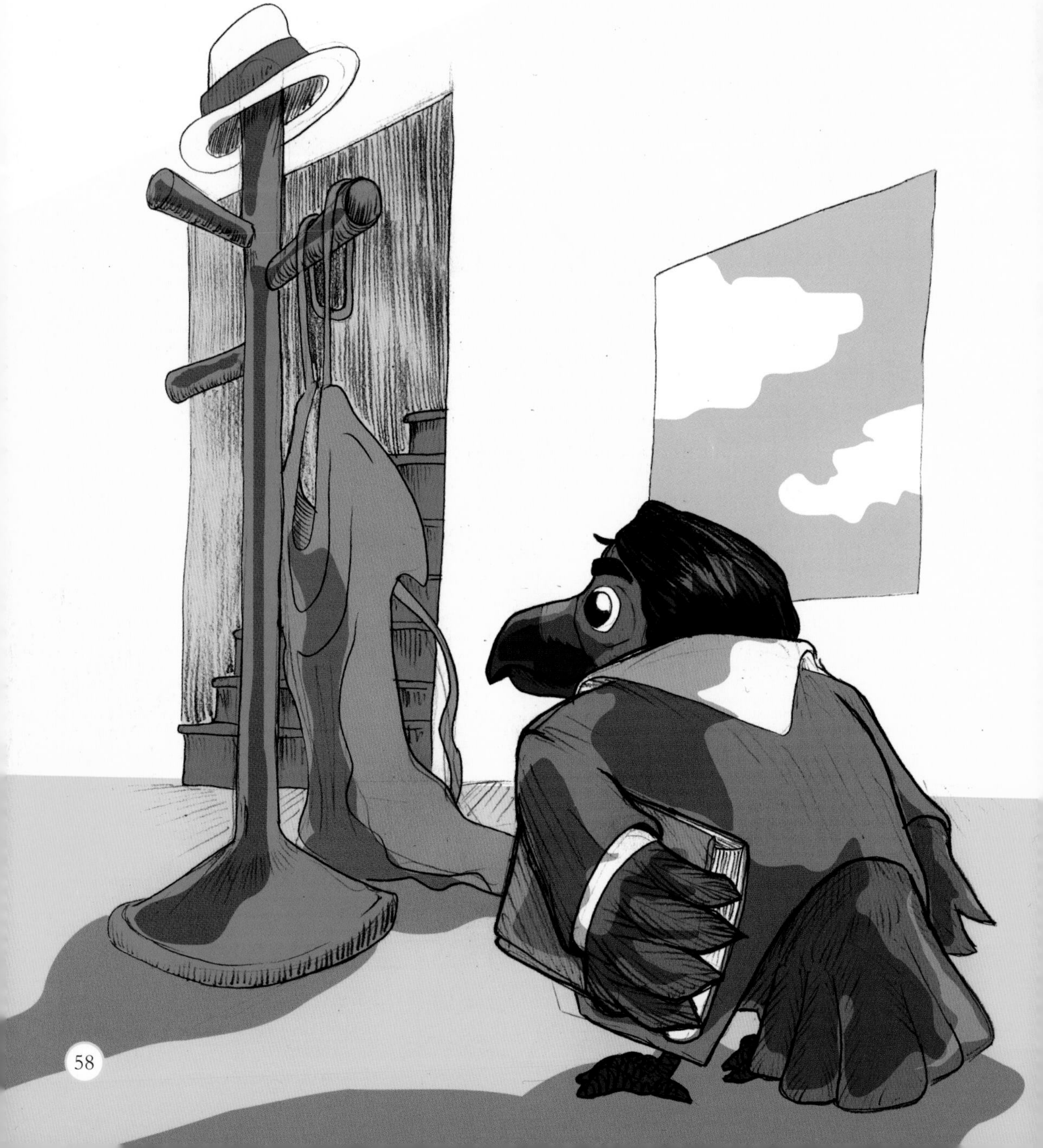

Connie said she'd learnt to make panna cotta.
Mama gave her the secret: rum, a whole lotta.
Everyone agreed with this plan
(Clemenza said he'd licked the pan),
So there was applause for the Don's daughter.

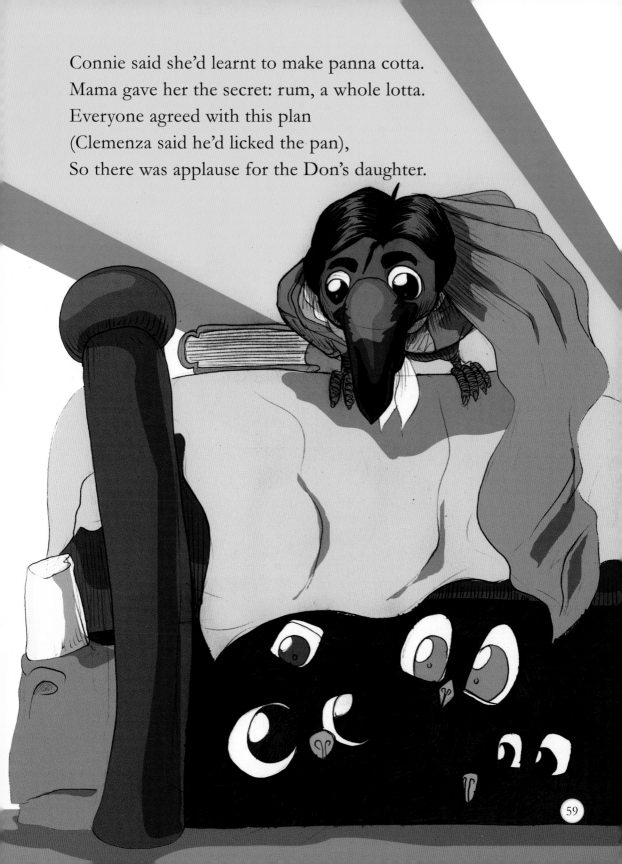

The morning of the Cake-Off
brought news to unsettle:

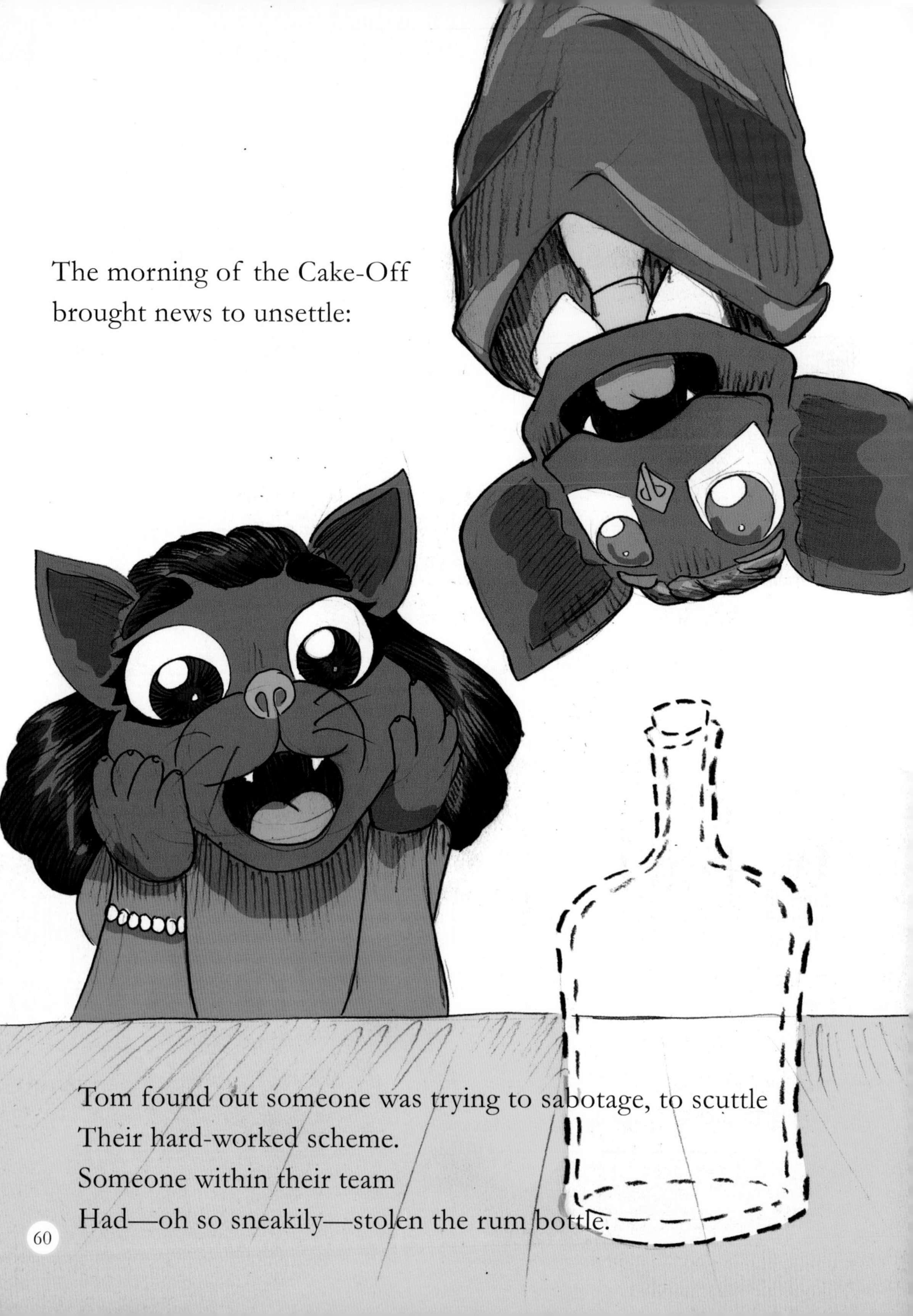

Tom found out someone was trying to sabotage, to scuttle
Their hard-worked scheme.
Someone within their team
Had—oh so sneakily—stolen the rum bottle.

'Not to panic,' Michael said. 'Time to get rushing!
I know what to whip up, but I need something.
Find me eggs and a cherry,
Go distract the judges, who look scary.
What would the Don do, we must be thinking.'

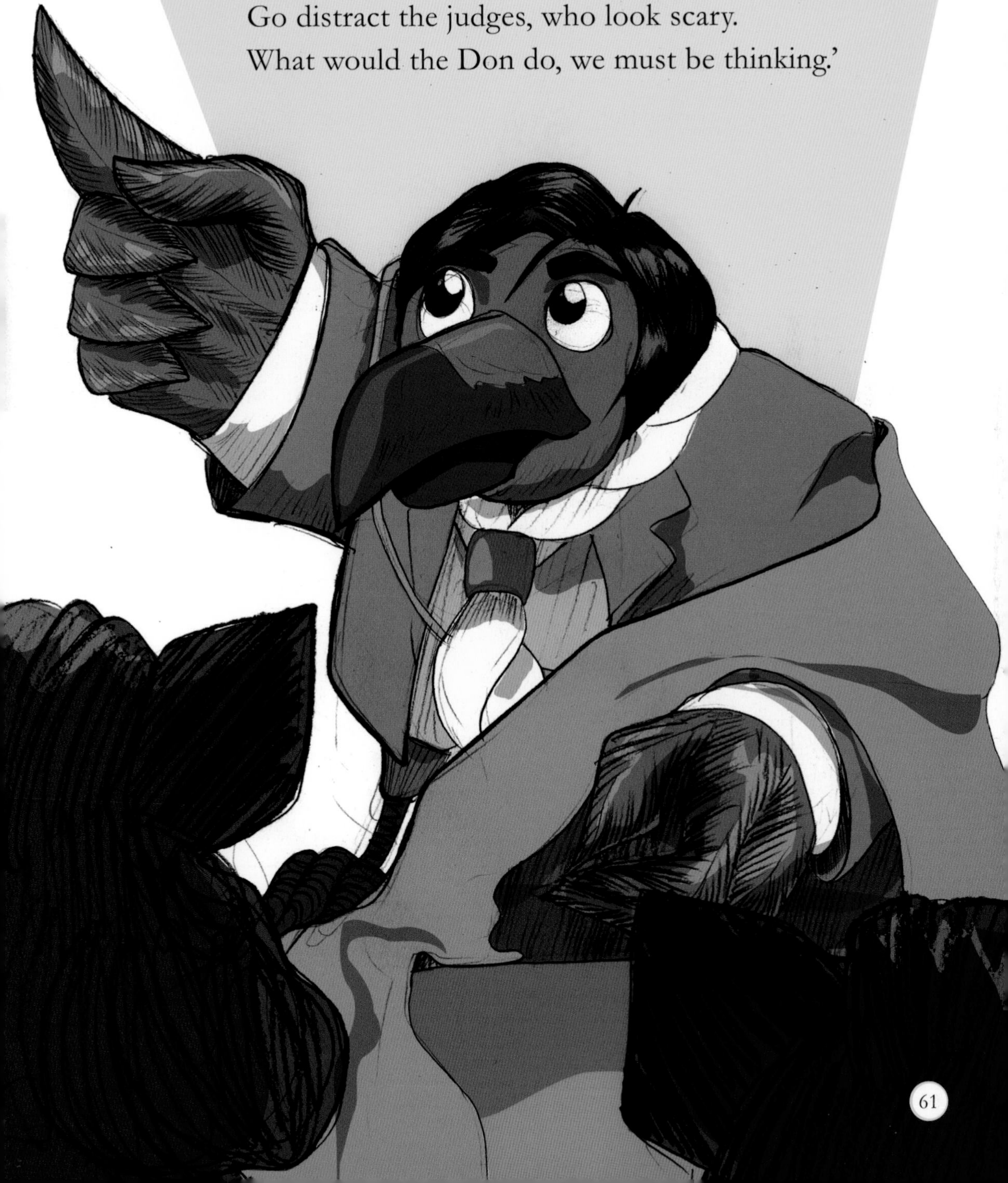

The judges were already tasting when the song began.
Johnny Prince warbled as Kay danced the cancan.
The judges couldn't help but look.
And Tom, carrying the cookbook,
Went and found enough eggs to feed all of Japan.

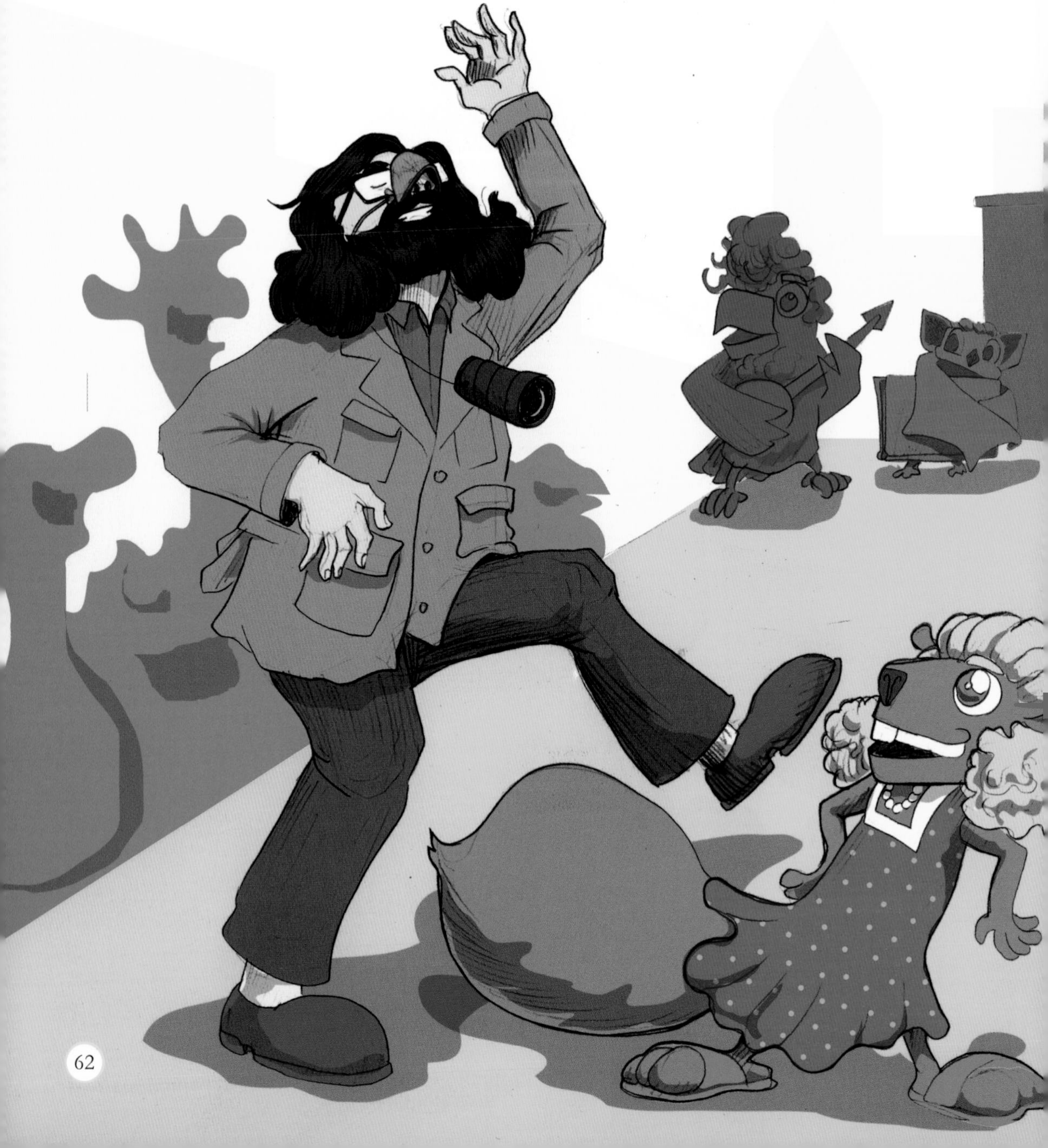

Michael cooked while the others started the hit.
Pies were placed on seats, candles were lit.

Shoelaces were tied together
With little strips of leather.
The scheme had been dreamed up with style and wit.

The song goes on
while the clock strikes disaster:

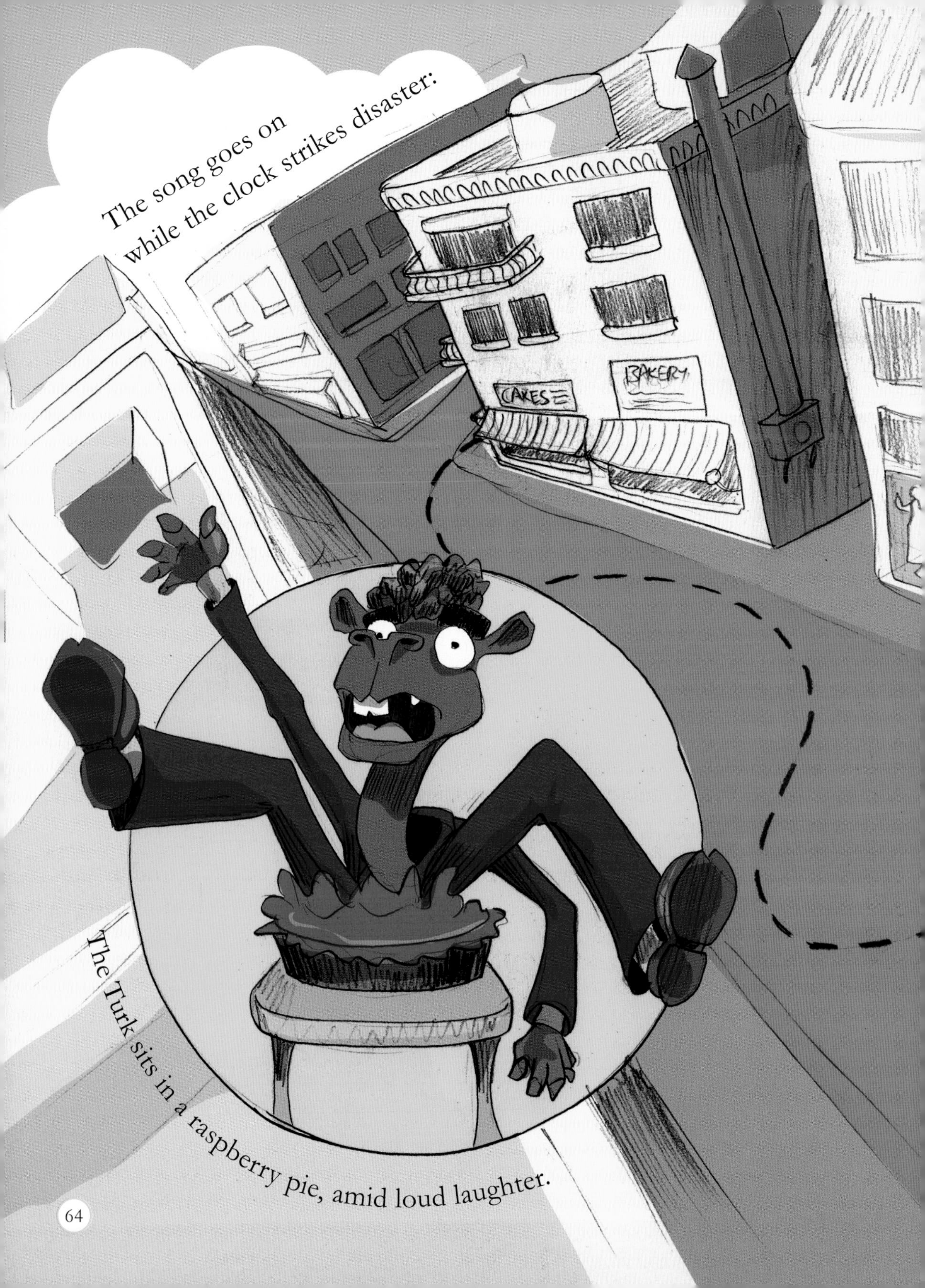
CAKES
BAKERY

The Turk sits in a raspberry pie, amid loud laughter.

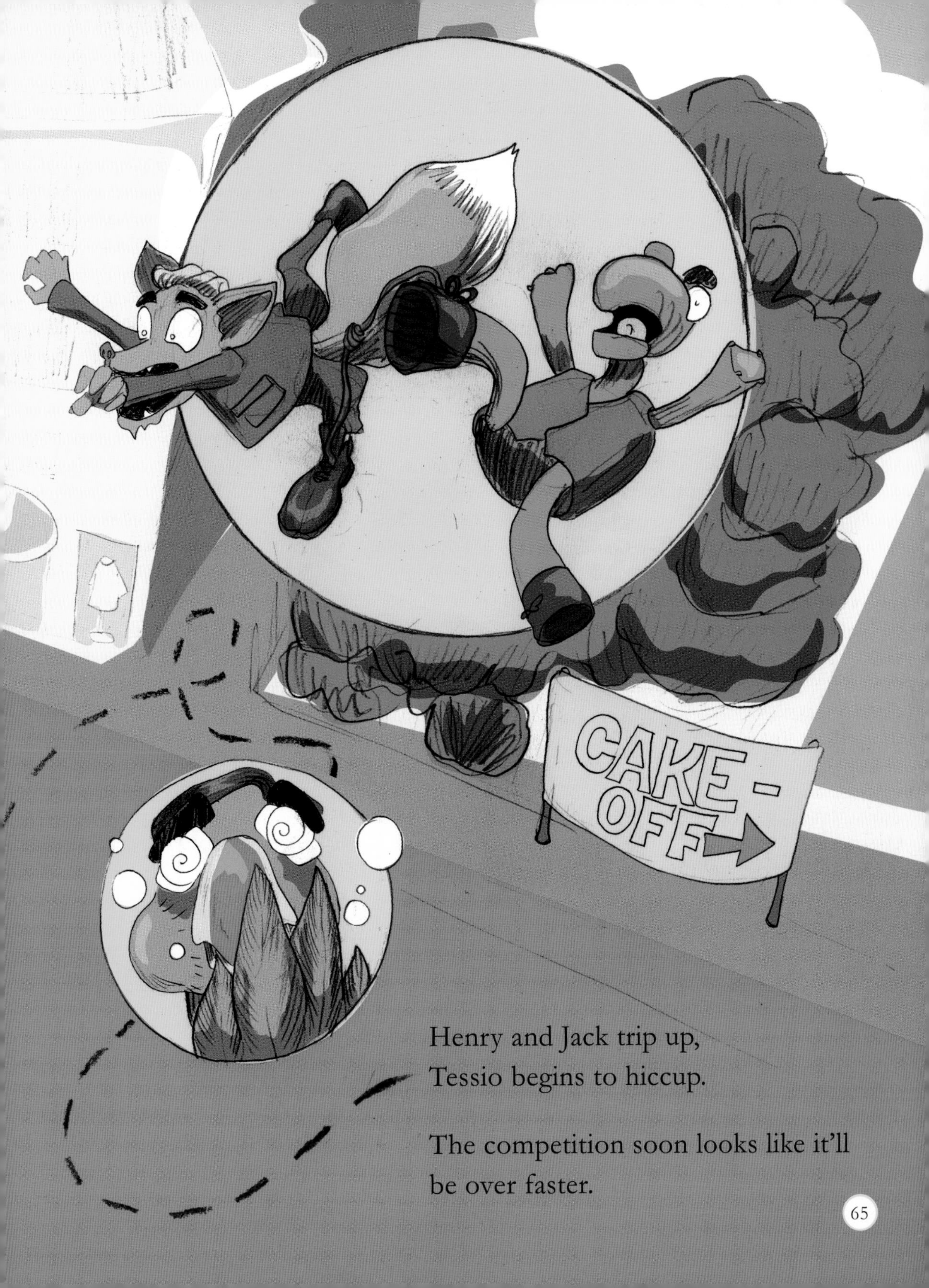
CAKE-
OFF

Henry and Jack trip up,
Tessio begins to hiccup.

The competition soon looks like it'll
be over faster.

Finally, Judge Francis came to try Michael's dish,
The kids crossed their hearts and made a wish.

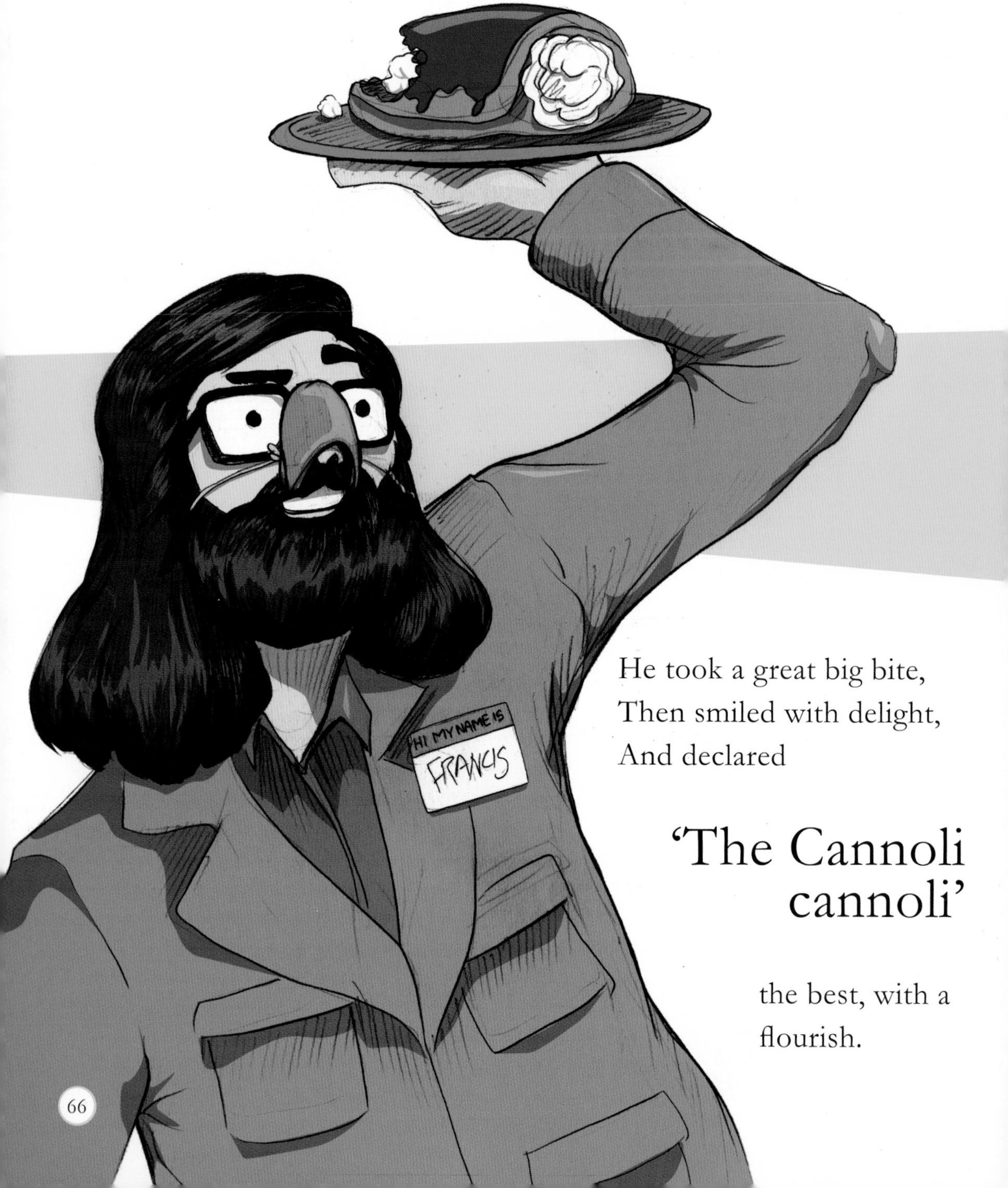
HI MY NAME IS
FRANCIS

He took a great big bite,
Then smiled with delight,
And declared

'The Cannoli cannoli'

the best, with a flourish.

After the announcement, the judge stopped to eat some more.

'Forgive me,' he chomped, 'but I must have at least four.'

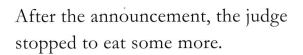

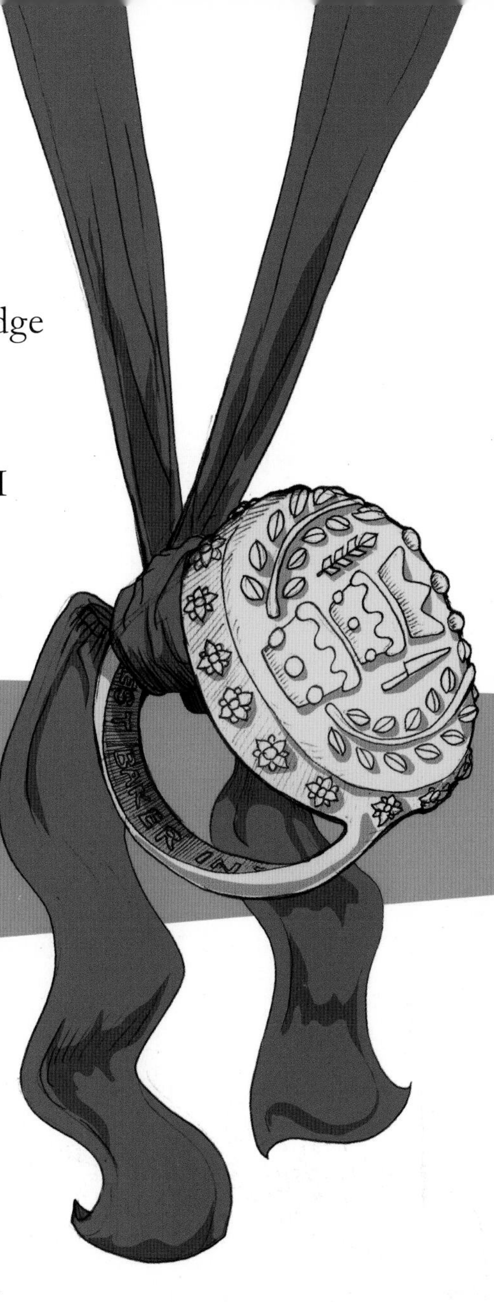

'But what of the hard candy?' Tom asked rather grandly.

'Oh, that,' grumbled the judge. 'It broke my tooth—it's still sore!'

Michael smiles with the championship ring on his hand.
Those around him kiss it lovingly, and they understand:
Though the apron may be loose,
He sure is wearing Don's shoes.
Without a doubt the young baker looks so grand.

As a merry gang with pastries in their eyes
Swings by and wonders what they cost to buy,
Michael gives them out for nothing,
Says, 'Remember, here's the thing:

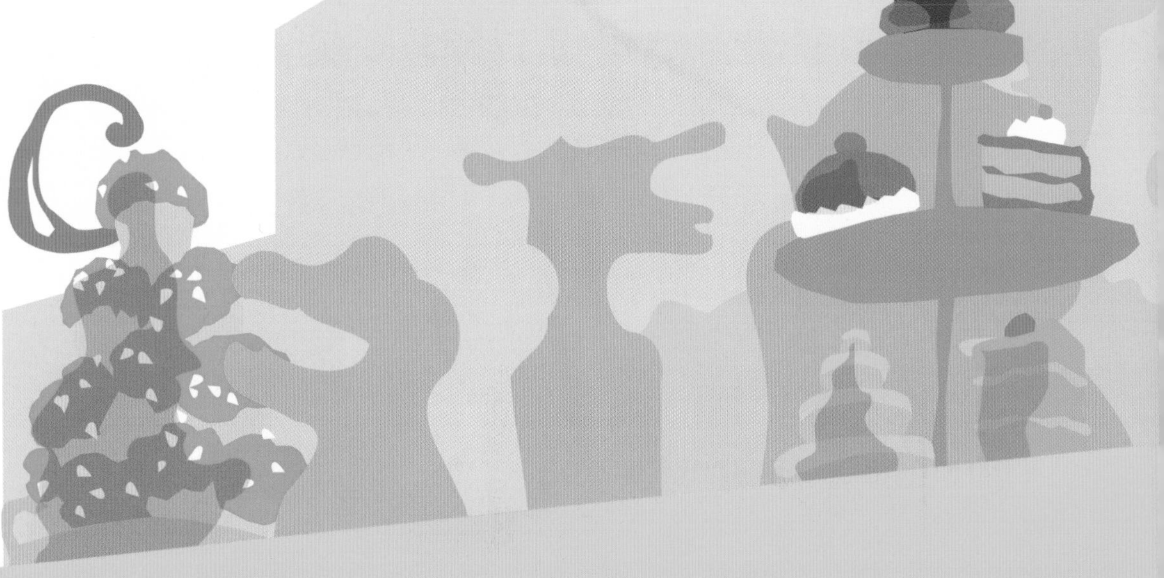

Just be nice to me
—and to all the guys.'

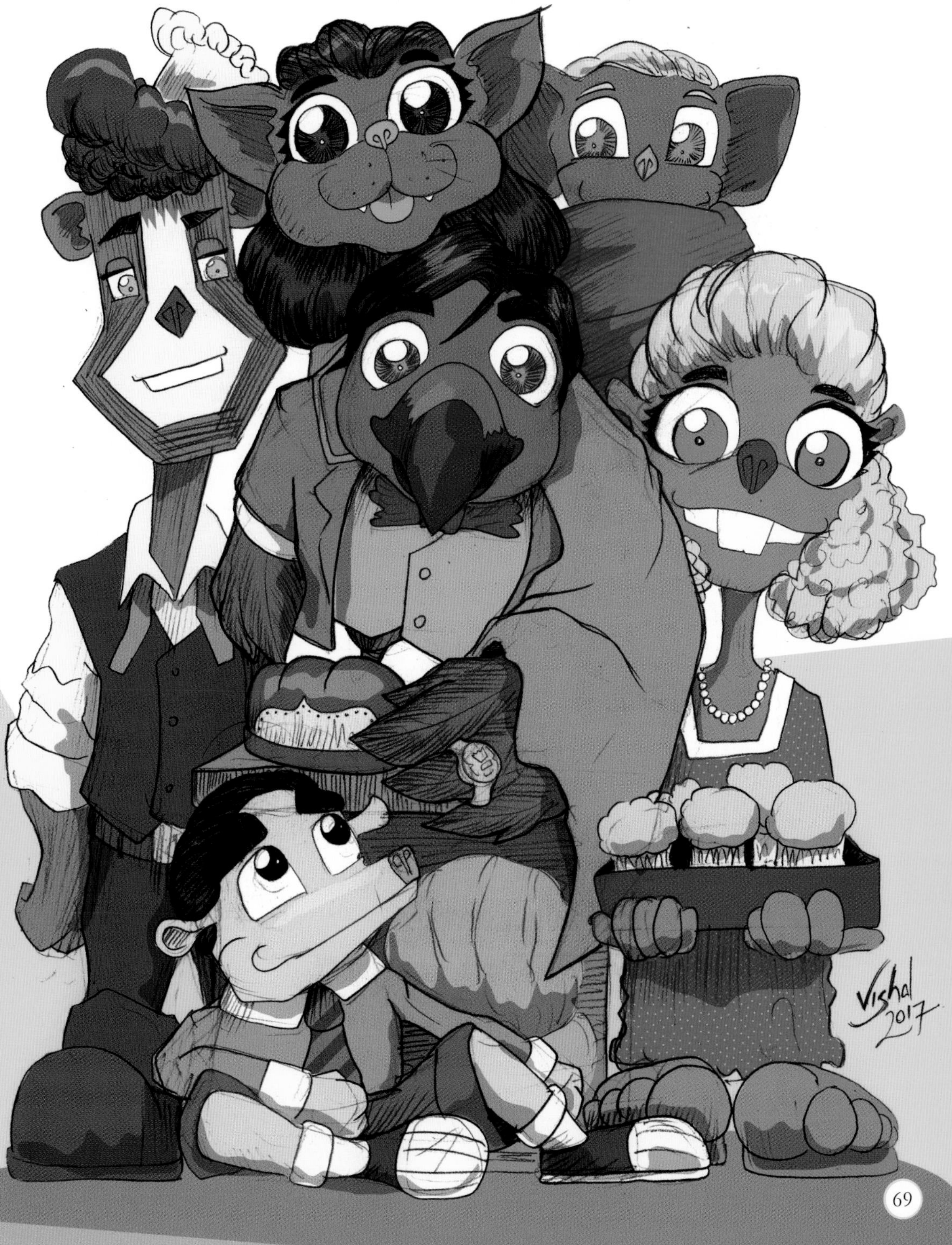
Vishal
2017

The Best Baker's Dozen

Friends and family

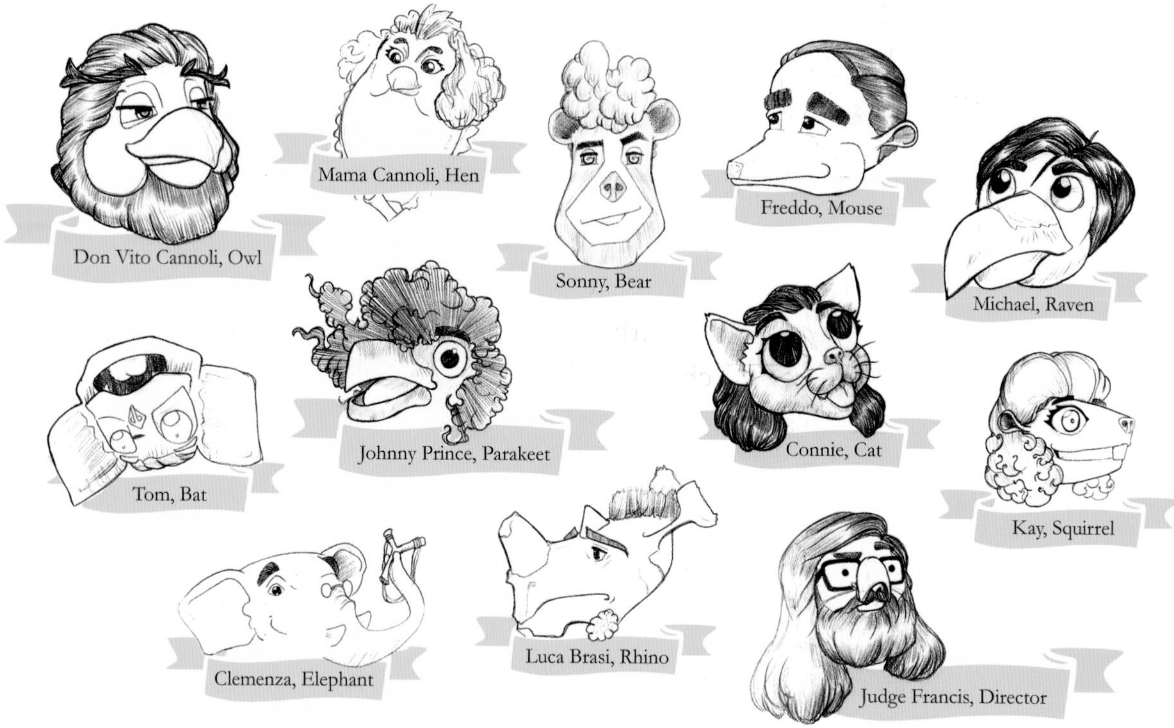
Don Vito Cannoli, Owl
Mama Cannoli, Hen
Sonny, Bear
Freddo, Mouse
Michael, Raven
Tom, Bat
Johnny Prince, Parakeet
Connie, Cat
Kay, Squirrel
Clemenza, Elephant
Luca Brasi, Rhino
Judge Francis, Director

And a few bad eggs

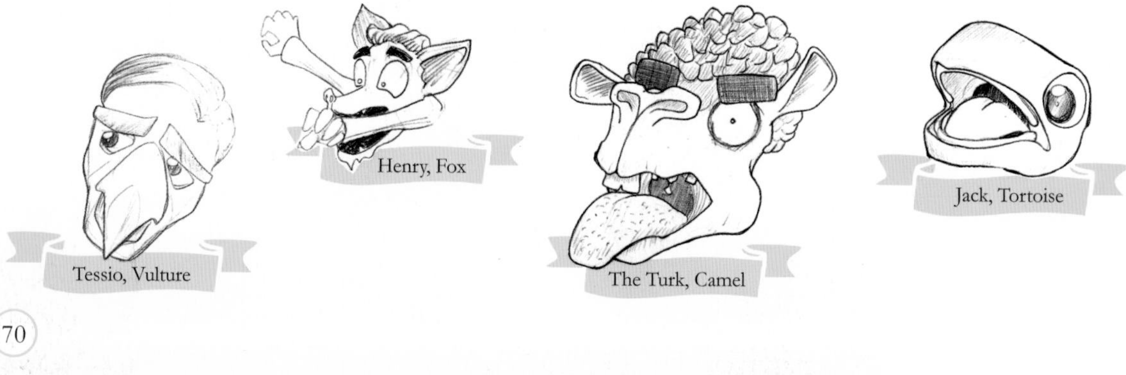
Henry, Fox
Jack, Tortoise
Tessio, Vulture
The Turk, Camel

Thank You

From *Tintin* to *The Odyssey*, I heard adventures before I could read.
This is for parents and grandparents who brought me up to speed.
My father, who showed me this film at an age too tender,
My mother, who never let relentless questions offend her.
I thank my fortune for this illustrator beyond compare,
Who finishes my sentences with pencilled flair.
My wife, for ruffling my hair and for cooing,
And, when needed, tut-tutting and shooing.
Poets Cohen, Seth, Cope continued to steer,
As my limericks dressed up in clothes by Lear.
Love to friends who enthused and cheered each peek,
And to those who checked if the paperwork was weak.
Last but not least these lovely Penguins I must here thank.
We can't all be Francis Ford, but at least they let me be frank.